Leaving Dahomey

Book One

Friendlytown

Trilogy

To my buddys, this one is for you...

JUDE SHAW

To Rick Smith

Jude Shaw AKA

Robert Harvey

1

Remembering

Evelyn Sedalia Shaw

Constance Aurea Jordan

THE AUTHOR'S JOURNEY

TO AND FROM DAHOMEY

Leaving Dahomey did not begin in earnest until five and a half years after I started it when I came across a novel by Frank Yerby called The Dahomean. I had been led indirectly to Dahomey by the late Nana Yao Opare Dinizulu while tracing his lineage to his ancestral home in Ghana—where he would become a Chief Akan priest before returning to America.

Once I started researching Dinizulu's homeland in south-eastern Ghana, I was just a stone's throw from a narrow stretch of land between Ghana and Nigeria: Republic of Benin or ancient Dahomey. Following Dinizulu led me to three great Afrikan Kingdoms, Ghana, Dahomey, and Nigeria. Early in 2011, I began focusing my research on southeast Ghana, Dahomey, and southwest Nigeria or the Bight of Benin—

4

where these cultures sometimes intermingled.

Yerby's novel is based upon an excellent anthropological study by Melville J. Herskovits: Dahomey: An Ancient West Afrikan Kingdom. Yerby called Herskovits' work a magnum opus. Herskovits includes the writings of anthropologists, sea captains, and agents of various European countries doing business on the Guinea coast. Yerby cites eighteenth and nineteenth travelers, including Sir Richard Burton, who was fascinated by Fon, the language of Dahomey; Bullfinch Lamb, an agent for a British trading company; William Smith, a surveyor for the Royal Afrikan Company; Archibald Dalzel, The History of Dahomey, published in 1793, provides a compilation of the works of the earlier writers; and J. A. Skertchly's Dahomey, As It Is, published in 1873.

By the end of the eighteenth century, Dahomey was the most traveled Afrikan nation by Europeans. They cited fantastic tales of wealth, the kings' extravagance, and battalions of women soldiers called Ahosi or Mino.

In May of 2014, my ninth year working on my manuscript, I came upon the scholarly writings of Chief Zogbe: The Sibyls: The First Prophetess of Mami Wata. Later that year, I came across another excellent source of information: Ana Lucia Araujo's journal: Dahomey, Portugal, and Bahia: King Adandozan and the Atlantic Slave Trade. Leaving Dahomey was also impacted by Dr. Francis Bacon's 1842 geologic study for the Royal Geographical Society of London on Cape Palmas, Liberia.

I pay tribute to Asadata Dafora of Sierra Leone. I learned about Dafora from Marcia E. Heard's dissertation: The Dafora Aesthetic, Technique, Intent, and Style.

In the 1930s, Ismay Andrews, a former Dafora dancer, taught East Afrikan dance in Harlem, USA. Michael Olatunji left Dafora to form an Afrikan dance company that introduced the dances of Nigeria. Nana Yao Opare Dinizulu (mentioned above) founded his dance company in 1848, based on his

work and that of his wife Alice Dinizulu
(Ohema Afua Owusua), a former Dafora
dancer. Alice Dinizulu was one of the select
few black dancers who were the cornerstone
of Afrikan dance.

CHAPTER ONE

It was October of 1841, and the ancient West African kingdom of Dahomey was ablaze. Once again, its people's lives returned to the normal round after another one of King Guezo's warring campaigns. It had been waged eighty miles north of Abomey against the Attahpahm people. Guezo had marched with thirty-eight thousand men and women.

It was a matter of course for the fifteen thousand soldiers of the standing army, including five thousand Ahosi, the elite female troops. But those who were not a part of the regular army, almost five thousand—and eighteen thousand commissariat followers—were just happy to return to their lives again as peaceful farmers, merchants, craftsmen, and artisans.

A soft breeze caressed the land, visible by the sway of the trees, and birds sang atop a baobab tree. For Adeoha and everyone else living in the village of Atogon, the harvest had ended, and the time of the palm trees to bear its kernels was near. It was a time of celebration, a time to thank the earth vodun for life, the sky vodun for rain, and the ancestors for their guidance.

Adeoha's life was filled with good fortune, one good coincidence after another. Need there be a reason, she thought, but truth be told, they're just ordinary events, no one can deny that. It's their frequency that astounds.

It all started with her dance of anticipation. After that, many people whispered the vodun were singling her out for some special purpose. Adeoha stood quietly beneath the palm trees. Such a simple tree, she thought, and they're everywhere in Dahomey. Everyone— commoner, noble, or royalty—owns the palm tree under which is buried their umbilical cord. For it is the guardian of our Fa, our Destiny.

Adeoha made her body rigid, clenched her fists above her head, took a deep breath, and pulled her three souls to her. One is inherited or ancestral, and she said a prayer to the ancestors asking for their guidance through the difficult times. The other, the Creator in her being. And her personality, which she will be held accountable.

A moon had passed, and the second rains had come, and the planting for the second annual harvest had begun. For Adeoha, her measure of labor for the day was finished. She walked in from the land of her grandfather, Ewansi. She fell behind her fellow workers, her eyes drawn to the children helping their mothers in the fields by keeping the birds away.

"They were people of no consequence according to the notables and others of high rank, Adeoha thought. They were the poor, the tenant farmers, the servants, and the slaves. Yet, they learn to survive and find joy in what little they have and not let misery or pain or suffering annoy them. Thus, in the end, we are all just people, Adeoha thought.

In another field, former slaves and their children were at work. "It is good that the lives of their children are not predestined. They will not inherit their parent's status as slaves. They can buy land and farm it, or choose another profession, or even marry into the household of their masters.

"One thing remains as before: the descendants of the slaves of Ewansi's grandfathers are obligated to work for him one-half of each day."

Adeoha dreamed of making a big name as a trader. She hoped that her deeds would be known in the great trading towns in Dahomey and the legendary lands of Kumasi and Benin. "I want to see these places for myself; I want to know how it is there, I want to match my skills against the best.

"It was not so long ago that I had no thoughts beyond living life idly by as a hammock-borne lady with status and a large inheritance of palm groves, cattle, and money. For the palm groves, I can thank my maternal grandmother, Lady Glyya. The sons would have inherited all, except for Lady Glyya's cunning and crafty maneuvering through the complex Dahomean legal system. I must learn about this legalism that Afrikans and tradition hold so dear."

As Adeoha walked on, the children were no longer in her sight, but they had stirred memories of her school days when the boys and girls her age were separated. She came to envy the boys, for they could sit in on the clan's big council meetings.

So, she crafted bold plans to get close enough to the boy's hastily built structures to eavesdrop on their secret conversations. Most of it was talking about their exploits with the girls her age. Sometimes they exaggerated so much, she almost burst out in laughter and revealed her hiding place.

The boys, at some point, would settle down to serious clan business and repeat what they had overheard. Personages of high rank—chiefs, priests, storytellers, diviners, and family heads often attended the councils. She slowly began to understand the world about her. But her childhood schemes became bolder on one occasion. She thanked both the vodun and Minona, goddess of women or whoever was responsible for saving her that time.

She had traveled with her family to the city of Allada for a festival given by her relatives. Upon arriving, she heard stories of a clan meeting among the big Dahomean houses that would soon take place. The members of the houses and extended houses were descendants of those who had held high office under past kings, and many now held office under King Guezo.

The people of Abomey had never before condescended to have their clan gatherings beyond Abomey. This meeting caused quite a stir among the inhabitants of Allada. The council from Abomey would meet at a compound not from where Adeoha stood.

"The people of Abomey see themselves as being better than us," a woman in the crowd said aloud. "We must listen to their arrogance about the splendor of Abomey, the greatness of their past, and the magnificence of their arts."

After hearing the words coming from the crowd, Adeoha could not help thinking, what an exciting challenge this can be. I will give anything to listen to a small measure of what they say. She found herself standing at the outer wall of where the council would meet. Eavesdropping would not be as simple as with the boys; it would take getting inside the house. There was nothing she could do, but the thought would not leave her.

Then a good idea came to her; Legba, take my breath, she voiced to herself, maybe I can do this. She reasoned that the members of the various clans are coming from all over Dahomey. Therefore, they can't all know each other. Her footsteps led her to the nearby marketplace, where she bought breeches and a shirt and cap in the boy's fashion of the day.

The next day, pleased with her disguise, she entered the compound, feeling she would not be noticed among so many. And now that she was inside, it was just a matter of blending in. She was awed by the long corridors covered with appliques heralding the deeds of individuals and clans.

She followed the men and boys into a large pavilion that she welcomed because it was a hot day. From there, she and the other boys were directed to their places and sat upon the ground. Adeoha was fortunate that the boys gave her no mind; instead, they were busy trying to impress the clan elders with their attention, so they sat without talking, their eyes affixed to whoever was speaking.

After a while, Adeoha sensed she had completed her task. She was not there to learn their secrets or anything like that. Her little prank was over. She saw an opportunity to leave as everyone was absorbed in a singer composing a new verse for the occasion. Then she saw one of the adults of importance approaching her, and he motioned to her to join the other young men now walking to another place provided for them.

The attitude prevailed in Abomey and Kana, the seat of Dahomean power, that the people from the provinces were not up to their standards, nothing more than commoners and peasants. Adeoha was a provincial, though no one could tell it from her speech or manners. Her father, Tubutu, had insisted she learn these things befitting the ways of kings and nobles.

She responded to the dignitary with the thick, aristocratic language of Abomey. The man believed the lad in his presence had come with his family from the great city of Abomey. After that, she was not set upon again. She heard fantastic stories and listened with particular interest to a young man and his stories about his clan.

She learned a great deal there, but how much she understood only time would tell. She had climbed the fortress of men and learned the things that were not the business of women. She would not repeat what she heard there, though she was eager to report the event to her first friend, Sewextu.

"Adeoha, we'll see you tomorrow," her fellow workers hollered to her from a distance, breaking her concentration. She waved back and headed off to meet Sewextu.

It was not long before Adeoha arrived at the edge of the forest. She sat down on the ground and leaned her head back on the sacred Loko tree. Sewextu was almost a sister to Adeoha. They trusted each other without a doubt, for theirs was a deep friendship formed at the beginning of their school days and tested many times. Sewextu, as her first friend, held specific ritual, religious, and legal obligations on Adeoha's behalf.

"When I have crossed the river and joined the ancestors," Adeoha would tell Sewextu, "it humors me that you will be the only one who knows where my cowries and valuables are hidden, and you will speak on my behalf at the will-reciting ceremony."

Adeoha smiled, recalling how often they got in trouble. Sewextu shared her spirit of mischief-making and adventure. They ignored the usual conventions and more than once felt the rod, though ever so light, leaving no scars on their dear backs.

Now for the first time, Adeoha is calculating her business potential on four fronts which would help her grow her profitable trading business into new markets: she included the money she had recently acquired from trading and lending, the added weight of her high status, her mother Lamtaala of independent wealth, and her father Tubutu whose wealth was surpassed only by that of King Guezo.

But more than all of that was her new popularity in many towns in Dahomey. She felt a strange sensation at that moment, it was like how you feel when you hear the loudest thunderbolt, but it was without sound. The feeling recalled one of the old stories she had heard many times without exception:

'When this happens, it is the voice of Maho, the Mother of Hevioso, the Thunder deity. She is letting you know important things await you, and it's not a time for folly.' Or perhaps it was her head telling her to have a good strategy before running off to Ugbiya, the most significant trading town in Dahomey.

She would soon turn sixteen years in age, and the big dry season had begun. According to the calendar of her yovo [white] friends, it all started twelve moons ago, or last December.

"I became a member of the Language of the Drums, the dance skills I learned there lead me to my new business, Adeoha thought. I gave a dance for Lamtaala's gybe to thank them for their guidance with my new business. Then, I danced in the competition against Allada, and because of it now, my name is whispered in many places in Dahomey, which has brought trouble to my family and me and my clan.

"And another matter, the language drum society is rooted in the oracle story. So the diviners and elders say my simple dance connects me to the oracle and the ancestors, and them to me."

######################################
###########

The short season of rain was longer than usual. Its waters ran deep everywhere, the rivers and streams, the wells and soil, leaving the second harvest plentiful.

Adeoha walked through the clearing and toward the village gate. A little later, she found Sewextu, waiting for her. Adeoha was highborn, so being chosen as her first friend was a great honor for Sewextu. The two girls embraced and walked toward the plantation of Adeoha's father. Adeoha noticed that Sewextu was unusually quiet and started to ask her if anything was wrong but decided not to interrupt her thoughts.

Adeoha and Sewextu laid on their sable bellies, looking out at the savanna and watching a pack of antelope scamper about in play. "Adeoha!" Sewextu said, ending the silence. "I will soon undertake a new adventure that I have long awaited."

"There is an air of mystery in your words," Adeoha said.

"I know you have always been aloof when it comes to societies in Dahomey," Sewextu said. Yet, when I stood before the council of the language drums, something came over me that I can't explain, and I said I could not become a candidate unless they agreed to accept you."

"I can't believe you did that,' Adeoha said. "Then again, I know you. There must be more to it."

"The language drum society rarely opens its doors to new initiates," Sewextu said. But now, there's an opening in the oracle story. Now is my chance to learn ancient lore and the tale and decide how to use them in verse.

"You are already making a strong name for yourself in storytelling and verse," Adeoha said.

"That is important to me," Sewextu said. "It seems my ancestors decided to give praise to the oracle. So now, that is my way in."

"But the oracle is a story for children," Adeoha said. "But we did have good times at the language drums compound when we were small.

"Yes," Sewextu said and laughed, "an oracle in each of us, let the ancestors be our guide. No impossibility cannot be overcome."

"I'm curious about their dance," Adeoha said. "They say the training is vigorous, and the exercises stimulate both physical and mental strength.

"I hope you can come before the council, or they will see it as an insult, it is a formality, and they will politely turn you down."

"You have a way out for me, as you have a way in," Adeoha laughed and said.

"You have not the bloodline or inheritance," Sewextu said.

"You have given me pause," Adeoha said. "If you find knowledge there, you will not be able to share it with me."

"Yes," Sewextu said.

"If I decide, I will present myself before the council at their pleasure," Adeoha said.

Sewextu knew Adeoha had decided to come before the council by her words.

Four days later, on Adjaxi, the last day of the Dahomean four-day week, Adeoha stood before the compound's high walls of the language drum society.

It was not so long ago when she was small, and with Sewextu at her side, they wandered at will through these same courtyards, playing games among the sacred trees of vodun legend. The palm and silk-cotton trees, the anya and loko trees, and the baobab.

As Adeoha waited, she thought about the priestesses and their only condition for allowing the children to play there was to listen well to the stories they told. Their best tale and the one with the best dances was the oracle. But what she and Sewextu enjoyed most, especially Sewextu—the priestesses encouraged them to tell their own stories.

Adeoha followed a young priestess beyond where she and Sewextu played as children, and down a path and through a gate, which left her riveted in another time and place; finally, the priestess slowed her gait and spoke to Adeoha:

"The earth you walk upon now is like the land where the oracle lives, a place that lays amid many trees," the young priestess said. "There its people have realms of stories to tell, as many as the leaves and their seasons."

Now Adeoha followed, and older priestess into a larger compound, that she had no idea of has a child, with wide-open spaces and hills, and majestic trees, shrines to Mawou to the east and Lissa to the west, and far in between Legba, Age and Gu; and the Great Gods Earth, Sky, and Sea Beyond the shrines she could see the houses of the priests and priestesses, each with their own courtyard, and the cult-house proper and its many courtyards stood out, where the candidates would receive instruction.

Finally, after a long walk around the compound grounds, Adeoha saw the other candidates, eleven in all, including Sewextu, who shot her curious look. She was taken behind a line of palm fronds and took her place with the other candidates.

The chief-priestess addressed each one in turn until she came to Adeoha. "This girl is called Adeoha," the priestess said, "daughter of Tubutu and Lamtaala. She wishes to come into our society. We welcome her to our soul-spirit, we welcome her to the rite of initiation, for the ancestors have guided her here."

Adeoha did not know what to say or think. She felt a certain kind of dismay for everything happening.

"The priestess—most of the priests of the language drums society were female— addressed Adeoha again, "You belong to the noble clan of your maternal grandfather. But it was your father's family that drew us to you."

And with that, Adeoha was accepted as a candidate for the rituals, taboos, and rites of oracle instruction.

Sewextu was awaiting her at the compound gate. "I can see you are not displeased with the way things have turned out, she said with great joy."

"This means there's a connection between our families, between our clans," Sewextu said happily. "We are the descendants of the Mami tradition, and our families from long ago through our ancestors have preserved our history, and without incurring the wrath of the Aladahonu kings."

"What does this have to do with them?" Adeoha said, for the remark bent her the wrong way. If that wasn't enough, Sewextu did not show the proper respect when she compared their families.

"It's nothing," Sewextu said; she had made a slip of the tongue, a measure of gloating. She was thinking about the wars between the Leopard Kings and the clans who opposed them.

"We have had good times here together at the storytelling sessions," Sewextu said.

"I use to listen so intently at the oracle story when I was small," Adeoha said. "Now I'm back here again.

"There were many points to the story and numerous ways of telling it," Sewextu said.

"When we were children, if our behavior was deemed inappropriate, Adeoha said in a humorous tone, our parents and the elders always found a way to have the oracle as moralizer or teacher."

"What does your mind say about what has happened today," Sewextu said.

"I will go see my father," Adeoha said, "for he is the only one who can explain this to me."

Adeoha belonged to the clan of her maternal grandfather, Ewansi; they were elevated to nobility by the Aladahonu Kings many years ago. Their stories were told to her while she grew tall, and it was their rituals and ceremonies and sacrifices and taboos she learned. There was no mention of her father's [Tubutu's] clan in Da's Belly, except the small stories he occasionally told her and her siblings.

Adeoha lay on her sleeping mat that night, searching her head. "How quickly change can come to one's life. The initiation is of short duration; besides, it will give Sewextu and me something to talk about in the coming years, our last great mischief together."

CHAPTER TWO

Adeoha would have to live two moons in seclusion within their cult-house and another seven moons in semi-seclusion after that. It reminded her of something Lady Nyeoye, a member of her mother's gbe or social club, had said on more than one occasion:

'We must learn to recognize the ancestors when it is, they who are guiding us to the crossroads of our lives—sometimes our battles can be long and difficult, and without the ancestors, we may never find our way.' The thought bemused her; first, nature's spirits, and now the ancestors.

"I'm an intelligent person, and it's going to take more than a few words by Sewextu and the language drums society to make me think that this is more than just a coincidence," Adeoha said.

"Now, my mind is on seeing my father," Adeoha thought. She left her mother's house, walked across the courtyard, and passed the eight huts of her father's minor wives to the master's bungalow. Where she found her father sitting under the shade of a large, applique umbrella as the wives attended him. "I have come to speak with you, Father mine," Adeoha said.

"Come under the parasol and sit on the stool," Tubutu said. Feeling the urgency in her tone, he dismissed his wives with a motion of his hand.

"What is it?" Tubutu said. It could not be that my eldest daughter has been chosen for membership in the Language of the Drums."

"As you have heard," Adeoha said. "I will soon begin the rites of initiation."

"I would not be good at my business," Tubutu said, "if I did not know what my daughter was up to—especially since it is being talked about all over Atagon."

"I have been chosen because of your tradition," Adeoha said. "How can that be possible?"

"Hmmm," Tubutu said. For what you seek, I am not as steeped in my family's traditions as other of my clan, but I will tell you what I can."

"That is all that I ask," Adeoha said.

"Tubutu stared at his daughter for a long moment. He couldn't help but wonder how the paths of Adeoha and the language drums society had crossed. It left him with a strange feeling, but it quickly passed.

"The stories of my ancestral clan are not spoken in Dahomey, Tubutu said, but the Language of the Drums has touched on some of it at times. He began thinking of explaining this to Adeoha because his family's three traditions came together at the great river Duwaya [the Niger]. But one of his clan traditions would be dangerous to his head, so he never spoke of it.

"I am of the xenu or clan of Dan Agrigom. My people are the Ga-Dangbe vodun of Ashante and Adja—Tado. Our spiritual forebears lived in this land, and it was called Amedzofe. Then the Oyo came and brought warfare, and after many years of fighting, our people grew tired of war and migrated to the regions of the Ashante and Mina peoples."

"When was that, " Adeoha asked.

"The time by the calendar given to you by the yovo you walk with," Tubutu said, "twenty-hundred years have come."

Adeoha said, nothing, like all Dahomeans, she could revel in a good story.

"The stories I heard as a boy," Tubutu said, "come from Adja—Tado and the groups that came there: Many of whom we have a kinship with, the Guin, the Ewe, and Fante peoples. The language drums could come from any or all of these places. I recall songs of verse telling when our ancestors lived in Ile-Ife, the spiritual homeland of the Oyo."

"The people of your story seem to have traveled a great deal," Adeoha said. "It seems too long ago to have an interest in my initiation.

"I was just trying to sharpen my memory," Tubutu said.

"My second tradition began when my grandfathers lived in the land of the blacks," Tubutu said. "Two influential kingdoms inhabited the region during their time there. They returned to trading along the Duwaya, but it took a while after their glory days in the big provinces on the desert's edge had ended.

"This is where I was during my childhood. My grandfather was called Ayawa. As his clan left the river and ventured closer to their ancestors' land, they began to sojourn and enjoy fishing in the rivers of Adja, where they found kin. It was on one of these visits that Ayawa met and married my grandmother, Mawuuli. She was Ewe from a family of high rank."

"They were my great-grandparents?" Adeoha said.

"The strength of blood or inheritance comes in five generations, according to the elders," Tubutu said. "After the marriage ceremony, they returned to Ayawa's home along the Duwaya. It was there I would spend wonderful days with my age-mates in misadventures. I remember listening to Mawuuli's telling about her mother being a Mami priestess."

"Legba take my breath," Adeoha said. "I could not have known this.

"Mawuuli is my grandmother," Tubutu said, "placing you within my five generations, as the elders say.

"Is there anything else you need," Tubutu said?

Spending this time with her father comforted Adeoha, not a small measure, for times like this, were not had often. Now she wanted to know more about her father's tradition.

"Father mine," Adeoha said, "you said you lived your childhood days upon the river Duwaya, and you were told the stories of a time when our ancestors were citizens in the land of the blacks. I want to learn about these times."

Tubutu had not spoken about his clan history to anyone. He had kept silent since his return to Dahomey twenty years ago. He had not even shared it with Lamtaala; he saw it as an unnecessary burden to carry, an innocent remark or utterance while sleeping could do great harm.

"I had dared not speak on this part of my family bwenoho, our true history," Tubutu said. "These stories are told not like at the storytelling sessions. I have never spoken of it, and you know what that means."

"Yes, Father mine," Adeoha said.

"The elders told me of the clan, Tubutu said: the hunters and their followers started in the direction of the King Mountains. They pushed on beyond the Yoruban lands, the Nago, the Mahi, and the Felaatahs. They braved many dangers from the local tribes and the great animals. Still, they pushed on and changed course many times because of high rivers, floods, and food scarcity. Still, they pushed on until they came upon an uninhabited forest. There it was, the great stories began.

"My memories are of an old woman sitting by the fire at night as the children gathered around her," Tubutu said.

"Sometimes her stories would explain life, other times right or wrong. At other times the tales were about clan legends, men and women of courage, who became our heroes. The woman was called Oyewo. She had a special way of telling; her movements and gestures brought her words to life, her timing and voice change left you leaning forward and your mouth wide open."

"I cannot tell her stories as well as she did," Tubutu said. But I will try to bring her voice to you as she did to me."

"'The great hunters knew the leaves and magic of the forest, Oyewo said. "'They possessed the skills to survive, the power of healing, and whatever else was necessary to defend themselves against the supernatural forces that would thwart them.

"'The aziza, the little people of the bush, assisted them, but only the most fearless hunters caught a glimpse of them before turning away. Our ancestors found peace in the bush for a while, but many wanted to leave and settle around the savanna's more familiar open plains. What they found beyond the forest was a great river that passes many rivers. As they traveled that river, one day, they came upon the feeling of a savanna nearby.

"'As time went on, the leadership of the various vodun groups fell to a woman called Kokwe. She pushed hard to explore the river upstream—for in this ancient time in our tradition, women-led. Kokwe was endowed with extraordinary divinatory abilities and healing power. There was much murmuring, and the people said they had no fear of the river and asked what the river could give them that the land could not.

"'Kokwe let it be known that the ancestors would guide them on a path that would find favor with Mami. So they braved the river and the elements until they could go no further. The people raised temporary shelters, and there they lived until the seasonal change, and the river was again passable. They repeated this many times.

"'At some point, the river flowed into a narrow gorge, and the river turned on them. The travelers were met with dangerous rock formations above them, precipitous rapids before them, and the swiftest currents yet faced. Lives were lost, and they ascended the rocky clefts above them and continued their journey by land.

"'In time, they reached a juncture where the river was again safe for travel. But from that time on, it was decided that only Kokwe and the bravest hunters would go ahead, and the others remain behind. Once the river was deemed safe, the rest of the group followed.

"'One night, when sleep came to Kokwe; Densu! Goddess of the waters came to her in a dream. Densu told Kokwe that it is when the river is high, it is navigable. She also told her, build sturdier boats and follow the river. It will lead you to a great city of riches and knowledge.

"'As time passed, sons became fathers, and fathers became grandfathers. The river became monotonous, and new hard days fell upon them, and they voiced many complaints. All the clans were in unison in saying, we should have settled on the land, there is no city of wealth on the river, and they began to lose faith in Mami.'"

"This was when Oyewo fulfilled the storyteller's art," Tubutu said, "at least to the nine, ten, and eleven-year-olds, as I was then. Oyewo would dawn a costume and dance with a new rhythm and played the drum, and she was in her last years. But you couldn't tell it. She'd leave the drum and swirl around and leaped through the air and settled to earth, and she becomes Densu, and she is speaking to Kokwe."

"'Even though the people have lost faith in Mami,'" Densu said, "'she is still protecting you as best she can and watching over those who believe in her and those that don't. She loves the way you're protecting each other, nurturing each other, and giving hope to each other. The river's hardships and your journey are not long at hand.'"

"The last story I heard from Oyewo, Kokwe crossed the river, and the line of descent fell upon Nubueke," Tubutu said. "Oyewo left the river with her clan and settled in another place. But I was older now. I came to a council meeting, now that I was old enough to take part. Can you imagine my surprise when the clan elder called upon a remembrancer? He recited the clan's predecessors and their adventures and exploits through time in a great city. The remembrancer began, thus:

"'On a day like any other, one of those cause and effect things that Legba and Fa like so well,'" the remembrancer said:

"'Nubueke and the advance party saw what looked like a bird splashing its wings in the waters in the distance. Within moments they realized it to be a young boy, and he was in trouble. As they paddled as fast as they could toward him, the current pulled him under, and he disappeared.

"'Nubueke jumped in after him and came up empty. The same thing happened again. He dived again and disappeared. Now, everyone knew that Nubueke had been under too long, and if he didn't come up soon, he had crossed the river. It was ironic that the brave Nubueke would give his life in a strange land to save a child stranger.

"'Just then, as all hope seemed lost, Nubueke came up with the boy's lifeless body in his arms. Once they reached the bank of the river, they placed the boy on the earthen ground. Nubueke began to drum on the boy's chest and had his medicine pouch brought to him. He took from it dry leaves and mixed them with what was necessary—ingredients of a secret nature—and this he placed about the boy's nostrils. The boy found his breath.

"'When the people from the country where the boy lived found him, the boy told them what happened, and they were astonished. So they brought Nubueke and his party to their country and feted them.

"The boy they had rescued was the son of a chief, a tall, stately man of some years, clad in a gold-embroidered robe, upon silk purple and green garments. The country was called Gao, and he was the chief of the Songhai nation.'"

The chief of Gao greeted Nubueke in celebration, "I am told you saved my son's life at great risk to your own."

"I could not have done less," Nubueke said.

"My son tells me he was fortunate that you found him," the chief of Gao said, "for you are not only brave, but you also possess the healing power of the forest."

"'For the next three days, Nubueke and his men were treated with hospitality and ceremony. And at night, when the moon smiles its light on the earth, the courageous Nubueke and the chief spent much time together consuming lixa from the same calabash, an honored custom among friends, and telling each other lore about the wisdom and courage of their respective clans. Finally, on the last night, the chief spoke of a city on the river's edge that caused Nubueke's heart to jump a beat.

"You describe a city much like Buktu in the land of the Mandinka," the Gao chief said. "My people know them well, for we have been adversaries for a long time. I will instruct you as to the proper manner and dress to present yourself and your people when entering the city, where perception and status are everything."

"'The next day,'" the remembrancer said, "'the Gao chief surprised Nubueke by giving him a sack of gold and brocades, and other fabrics for the cloth workers among his people in preparation for entering Buktu. '"

"You will need these things to present a good show," the Gao chief said. "You do not want to be looked upon as beggars."

"I will be forever grateful to you for your brave deed and your compassion concerning my son," the Gao chief said, "and I bid thee accept this small gift."

"'The Gao chief presented Nubueke with a jeweled dagger with a silver blade, hung upon a chain of gold, and its sheath made of embroidered gold and rubies.'"

"I thank you, my lord," Nubueke said. "It is an honor. My gratitude is beyond mere words, and I humbly accept this gift you have bestowed on me and my people and the knowledge you have shared with us on the face of my journey's end."

"'Nubueke and his party returned to their people and told them what had happened, and the king had sent two of his ablest warriors to help them explore the river's backwaters,'" the remembrancer said.

"'The people were moved when Nubueke told them there indeed was a great city on the bank of the river and its wings spread inland as far as the sky.'"

"Maybe this will put an end to our journey," some of the people murmured happily."

"Perhaps this means we can find land to work and raise a village," a man and woman shouted.

"'Nubueke and a small party went ahead to where the river widened,'" the remembrancer said.

"'Their search took them deeper and deeper into the bush. They placed men at intervals and left markings on trees and rocks to help them find their way back.

"'After two moons, their search seemed hopeless. But they pushed on across a long stream and walked on land to a hill. They climbed it and saw an inspiring stretch of land where they could live. The land was inaccessible except for crossing the stream and climbing the mountain and offered excellent protection from visitors or invaders.

"'Nubueke and his men, some fifty strong, set out for Buktu, leaving the remaining members of the group—five-hundred men, women, and children—at the established secret place. They entered Buktu as wealthy merchants in all the show and glory they could display in the yovo year of 1325.

"'When they arrived at their pleasure, they discovered the whole region filled with wealth and opportunity. A place that begins and ends with long caravan trails across the desert hauling the world's wealth, where work was plentiful, and life enjoyed under a single system of trade and law.

"'The group did well there in all manner of occupations and jobs: The building of mosques and libraries and schools was everywhere. The gold and salt trade on the river made for a hefty living, and in no less, the book trade and others had eating and art establishments.

"'The sultan Moussa was the ruler at the time our grandfathers arrived in Buktu. The sultan had not long returned from a pilgrimage to the Islamic city of Makkah. His procession included eighty-thousand people, and a thousand donkeys weighed down with gold.

"'As time passed, the sultan began sending young people from the land of the blacks to study at madrasas or universities in places called Cairo and Tunis. Our grandfathers tell stories of their adventures and times in other places called Morocco and Egypt.

"'As time will tell, our forefathers began to travel to these faraway places across the desert, not to learn but to teach. As a result, they were the highest teachers in their respective branches of learning in these countries.

'"Our ancestors heartily laughed at night around their open campfires after recalling the Arabian savants who came to visit their madrasas—some of whom found they were not equal to the rigid requirements of the black scholars. Thus, the most learned men of Islam could not believe that these black Afrikans were on a level with their Arabian counterparts.

'"Many, many seasons later, one of our kin as lore has it, called Kweisi, on business visited Goumbou in the land of the blacks. Kweisi happened to share the road with a Goth. They talked and eventually became friends.

'"The Goth told Kweisi he had come from Spain, passing through several dessert kingdoms to seek a new life in the land of the blacks. He called himself al-Keuti, the Goth. Later, he introduced Kweisi to his friend Mamari. The three became good friends, shared good times, and drank from the same calabash.

'"As it was, al-Keuti married Mamari's sister, and Kweisi appeared at their wedding wearing the jeweled cutlass passed down to him through the ages. Mamari immediately recognized it by the Songhai inscription, and called everyone to his side, and told them about the legend of the jeweled cutlass given to a passing stranger who saved the life of the king's son.

"'Kweisi, wisely presented it as a gift to Mamari who soon would come to the throne of the Songhai nation and rule over the land of the blacks. They exchanged a sword and sheath. Numerous royal doors were open to our forebearers during their rule.'"

"That's the story," Tubutu said, "from Oyewo, the storyteller to the clan's remembrancer."

"That was a long ago, father mine," Adeoha said.

"Yes," Tubutu said. After the remembrancer's recital. The rest of the story was told to me by my grandfather's while traveling the road."

"What is this university you speak of?" father mine.

"It's a school," Tubutu said, "not unlike the one you attended in your childhood. The difference is that it can extend from the age you are now until your adult years and beyond."

"What can they teach you that will take so long to learn," Adeoha said.

"Aahhh, you can learn all sorts of things there," Tubutu said. "These schools can be thought of like the stars in the sky, for each star carries within it a body of knowledge."

"Now I know the origin of your wealth and the history of your clan," father mine," Adeoha said.

"Yes, I inherited the ways of making a great wealth in the footsteps of my ancestors," Tubutu said.

"I understand why you have not spoken of this before," Adeoha said. "I will not speak of it again." But, as she spoke, she couldn't help but think of Sewextu and how she would have enjoyed telling her about Tubutu's tradition.

Adeoha left her father thinking, for him to voice the tale he just told me would lead to the immediate loss of his head. He could not speak of a country not far from Dahomey, where men raised magnificent dwellings for prayer and schools, where blacks can read and write their own stories, and people come from all over the Moslem world to study under black teachers. A story like this would make the Aladaxonu Kings and Dahomey look small in the people's eyes—and this could not happen in Da's Belly.

Adeoha's heart was filled with joy as she skipped through the compound and home.

CHAPTER THREE

They, all twelve of them, Adeoha and her sister-initiates, would spend the next two moons in the cult-house and its environs. Away from their family and friends.

The public ceremonies for the society of the Language of the Drums and reception for the initiates concluded. Now, the long days and intense training began.

Adeoha's first days were not what she expected. They started before the sun cast the first glow of a new day, the long warm-up exercises in the morning, and again at mid-day, and again at dusk. On one of these occurrences, a young priestess addressed the group in one of the courtyards.

"Soon, you will begin the same course of training as the priestesses of the society have before you," the priestess said. "However, before we begin your instruction's ritual and ceremonial phase, we will teach you to attune your body and mind as one.

"You will accomplish this through a series of isolation exercises that we hope will give you the fluidity required for our dance. What we desire is that you acquire the manner to apply specific muscles in your dance that will affect the onlooker with the illusion you're walking on water."

Adeoha and Sewextu sat in the courtyard of the cult-house. The night had come, and all they wanted was to rest their weary bones and sleep.

"So far, everything is about warm-up and exercise. I think it's dull," Adeoha said.

"Did you not say that the appeal for you is in the rigor of their dance training," Sewextu said.

"You are used to this," Adeoha said, "because you are a dancer by occupation, but I am not."

By the night of the fourth day, the exercises had rendered Adeoha and her sister candidates where they could do little else but fall upon their sleeping mats and welcome sleep. Adeoha was dozing off, but she could hear what she thought was the drum tempo and the voice of a priestess speaking in mellow rhythms—start with the head roll—eight to the right and eight to the left—rotate the head forward to the right and back—and forward to the left and back.

"I had a dream last night," Adeoha said. "A rather nice dream," and she proceeded to tell Sewextu about a voice giving her instruction. Then she stopped for a moment and laughed, "the ancestors visited my dream in the flesh."

"This place has changed your views somewhat, well, at least about the ancestors," Sewextu gibed at Adeoha.

"You know how dreams are," Adeoha said. "They jumped into the hand, wrist, and finger exercises, then they did the body stretch and body ripple to perfection, and ended with a beautiful ceremonial dance."

In the coming days, the initiates took turns showing off their new dance techniques before each other. Adeoha's technique did not bring the illusion she sought after several attempts.

Adeoha was the only one who did not pass the first phase of training.

"I can't do this," Adeoha whispered, "and considered leaving the compound as she looked at Sewextu.

Sewextu imagined her frustration and pride, knowing Adeoha always prevailed in any contest or challenge she entered.

"You have not faced anything as difficult before; you will get through it," Sewextu said.

"So much stress is put on bending the knees in different places," Adeoha said.

"Yes," Sewextu said, that's the starting point for all the dances. But it will come to you soon, and you'll wonder what the fuss was about."

The next day in the early afternoon, if she didn't have trouble enough, Adeoha was told to go to one of the cult house's inner compartments. When she arrived, an older priestess greeted her about Lady Glyya's age.

She began to play the drum and motioned Adeoha to begin the dance exercise. The priestess's voice was soothing, and she beat the drum tempo at intervals; the movements of Adeoha's legs and knees in the dance sequence found accord. Soon she passed the first phase of training and rejoined her sisters of the oracle.

Two graduate priestesses demonstrated the proper dances and rhythms to commune with the ancestors. First, each initiate danced with an instructress, beginning with the slowest beat and building to the highest dance cue associated with the drum tempo. Then the graduates pushed the initiates to sit and told them to see and learn.

The graduates began their dance by shifting from one foot to the other while swinging their arms from side to side in a rhythmic flow. None of their movements seem even, yet their dance steps are always on the beat.

The initiates are astounded, and they watch as the drummer builds to a fast rhythm. Then, the priestesses whirl into another dance, adding the manipulation of the arm and shoulder muscles, drawing the illusion of floating and the earth moving below their feet.

Later, when the sessions' exercises and dance training had ended, Adeoha and Sewextu sat in the darkness of night on the edge of a grove of cotton-silk trees.

"The dance of the priestesses was incredible," Adeoha said. "I could never learn to dance like that, but you will, Sewextu."

"For me, it's their verse; there will always be those with cowries who want this for their family history in song, " Sewextu said.

"The society has shown good judgment the way they keep the oracle story in the people's thoughts," Adeoha said. "When people see the magic of the dance, they cannot help but recall the oracle story."

"There are other secrets to the oracle myth," Sewextu said. "The diviners and priests tell them. Some chronicles are secrets of the elders concerned with the society's ancestral rites. The verse sequences are what I want to learn. They can take the popular story of the oracle from the tale or heho to the more significant myth or hwenoho."

During the next moon, the initiatives were taught the dance of commemoration, a testament to the ancestors and the oracle.

"What is this story about the dance of anticipation?" Adeoha said.

There has not been a dance of anticipation since who knows when in Da's Belly, " Sewextu said.

*****

The big day season has left the land dry, and the sun is low in the mid-afternoon sky; The opening ceremonies of the three-day event are in hand. The members of the language drums society have planned each day to be more lavish than the one before. It has always been this way, and the people have come to expect it.

The candidates will not appear on the first day, but they are ready, in both their physical and mental presence, after two and a half moons in seclusion in the cult-house proper. Slowly the people began to mingle in the flat public spaces within the compound. By late afternoon, the guests of the society, and family and friends of the initiates, were seated in the reserved area on mats in the trees' shade, on the hilly public space surrounding one side of the dance enclosure.

Among them, Adeoha's family, her father, Lord Tubutu, her mother, Lady Lamtaala, her grandmother Lady Glyya, her aunt Lady Owusua, and her brother and sister O'Gwumike, and Oshun, and her brothers and sisters of a different mother.

Only the priests and priestesses, graduate priestesses, and initiates who completed two or more seasons performed. The chief-priestess led a procession around the various shrines and sacred trees within the compound (under an assemblage, of a score, of gaudy umbrellas [some eight feet in breadth to twelve feet in spread], each with hanging applique cloths indicating their tradition and the deeds of men and women of their designation, within the language drums society.

They stopped with songs and chants, danced to the drums' rhythms in twos and threes and groups, and proceeded around the shrines and trees three times.

Next, the graduate priestesses wearing crimson cloths sang the Mawou-Lissa and Legba songs; three would dance at one time, the others carrying on in solo or chorus.

The candidates watched eagerly from the enclosed courtyard where the cult house was located (out of view of the spectators).

"I do not see your grandfather, the xenuga [elder clan head] of your clan," Sewextu said.

"Lord Ewansi and Lord Ajatauvi will not attend; the reason is political," Adeoha said.

"I have heard that one has come from afar to perform the initiation rite," Sewextu said. "She is a Mami Wata High Priest."

"I am not surprised," Adeoha said. "I have learned during my time here that the vodun tree has numerous roots and branches," Adeoha said.

"They say she has the gift of divination and healing," Sewextu said.

*****

The next day, through the majestic trees of the compound, a cloudless, blue sky was visible, heralding the second day of ceremonials which would begin just after mid-afternoon and be completed by moonrise.

The guests and family and friends were present as they were the day before. But today, the spectators came in great numbers and with their children according to tradition.

As they entered the first compound and the second compound as they had the previous day, a new display on the fringe of the dance enclosure appeared. As they got closer, it became clear they were on the verge of something special; a four-sided display of large applique cloths hanging to the ground, each one held up by two poles eight feet in height, given a breadth of six feet.

Two graduate priestesses met the crowd and informed them that the displays represented the ancestors who, from time extending back beyond memory, have carried the story of the oracle in their hearts and minds and passed it down for future generations.

The ornamented displays were applique cloth composition, consisting of various colors and designs of people walking the earth and sky, clad in togas and other native ware of red, blue, and purple, and throughout, picture stories of elephants, lions, birds, and crocodiles, amid beautiful landscapes, rivers, and mountains.

The people enjoyed the crafts, and their children were having fun with the black elephants, some with green ears and yellow tusks, and blue lions and yellow birds, all blending in with red Afrikan men. The patterns slowly drew larger through time.

"These appliques could only have come from skilled workers of the cloth sewing guild in Abomey," a man's voice was heard to say. "What we have here is expensive and take a long time to make, so the society must have friends in high places," another man said.

"The needleworkers are very much aligned with royalty and see themselves as having the favor of the king and nobles, A second man's voice was heard to say, "and there's no love lost between the clans of the Leopard and Serpent."

The first man spoke again, "it's hard to imagine the cloth-sewers risking their position. They see themselves above commoners. But again, they are needed. Who else can dress the gods and upper-class Dahomeans."

After a while, when everyone had seen, remarked, and delved into the display, the priestesses informed the crowd the rest of the ceremony would begin soon.

The festive mood of the spectators continued when they caught sight of the candidates, dressed in fine green cloths, as they emerged from the cult house led by two priestesses into the dance enclosure and seated on mats.

As the Mami ascended the high platform, made for times like these by the language drums society, she was ready to address the candidates. Few in the crowd had ever seen a Mami Wata Vodun High Priestess** (the powerful water spirits), but most knew their calling. So many among the onlookers edged closer to hear her better.

"I am Mama Ezogbo," she began. "For some of you, seeking initiation, this will be a crossroad, a new beginning in your life, measure it well like my proverb tells: If the Great God sees you, then you are tired."

"We are of the Mami vodun clans. They are our ancestors, and we are their sons and daughters. The Mami Wata was also known throughout the old world as Isis, Ephesus, and Rhea, among her holy names.

**Mami Wata: Africa's Ancient God/dess Unveiled Vol. 1 &. 2 ~ By Mama Zogbe

"The Sibyl matriarchs were the first oracles and prophetesses during that time, and that is when the oracle's prophecy began.

"Beyond that," Ezogbo said, "the oracle reveals nothing and says nothing about its purpose, only that within its land lies all that is necessary to fulfill the tasks of those who need its guidance or seek it. The ancestors have carried this story through time, and one day they will guide us there.

Adeoha's eyes could not help being drawn to Ezogbo; she wore a green robe and head-wrap of native cloth. The jewels she wore had an impressive shine. Her movements were stately.

"I have just completed a fascinating journey across land, water, and dessert,"

Ezogbo said. "There are things I had commonplace with that I'd like to share with you.

"I crossed the Duwaya River with my guide and his men; we traveled deep into the land of the blacks. It was a scorching journey that lasted two moons. It was there I met as planned a priestess of the Fulbe vodun clan. She asked me to initiate her into Tchamba because she wanted to free her ancestors who sold fellow-Afrikans into slavery.

"The Fulbe priestess made ceremony on behalf of her ancestors who sold other Afrikans into bondage, and they are now free from the never-ending chaos of the middle world. They, in turn, are now obligated to find a remedy for their victims and help them find their way back to their ancestral clans.

"It is the same for all people of the earth, Afrikan and non-Afrikan. The people who have inherited wealth from the enslavement of Afrikans live in a forbidding world; Tchamba knows that their descendants are not responsible for what they have done. But, at the same time, the spirits of innocent Afrikans who have suffered violent deaths, like their tormenters, have no peace and are trapped in spiritual captivity forever.

"Tchamba is as old as Afrika herself. It is the heritage of all men and women. You may have ancestors involved in or suffered from the slave trade, regardless of race or color. I ask you to come and join Tchamba, a system of divine restitution and compassion and rescue your ancestors so that their souls may find peace. For doing so, you and your family and your ancestors will be blessed, rewarded, and protected— the road is open."

"There is another story I would like to leave with you," Ezogbo said. I have long been occupied by the world's many cultures and how each has so much to offer.

"Then, one day at first light, I could see a long stretch of hills as high as the clouds extending as far as I could see. I did not think about it until my party encountered a group walking toward us. My guide informed me that they were known as the Habe people, and their home was atop the distant hills—as he pointed to the same place that had drawn my attention earlier.

"The men said they were returning from visiting kin. We camped together for the night, and they revealed a holy man among them. We prepared our huts of branches and fraternized. I paired with the Habe priest. We were of the same quarter, and I was interested in what he might say.

"He talked about his people's creation stories. I listened with the utmost respect. He spoke of his tradition and the sacred words passed down of sky beings who visited his ancestors.

"They came in a vessel that left a trail of fire and stirred a high wind and made the sound of thunder. The Habe priest described tablets in the ground with drawings of water deities in human form and how they instructed his people about the nature of the stars and the measure of the sky.

"The priest's story in its description had a familiar tone. I recalled a similar story by a passing storyteller. But there was more to cause me to wonder when I asked the priest about his ancestors, he pointed to the east and spoke of the visitor's home star, and it cast a red glow of light through the temple and upon their sacred altar.

"The priest's words recalled memories of my childhood in Mami instruction; and a story of a red beam of light shining from the heavens that transformed on the temple's altar into the Divine Mother Goddess.

"Before Ezogbo continued, she turned and looked at the temple consecrated to Loko and then to the initiates.

"Loko is the Vodu of the trees, and the trees that live about us have souls, though not like the souls of men. Their essential nature is magic and healing. So we connect magic and healing with the story of the oracle.

"Our ancestors are spirits, and their souls need nourishment too, so laden them not only with your thoughts and love and prayers but with your resolve to keeping the story of the oracle alive for future generations in memory, shrine, ritual, and festival."

The chief priestess led a small procession, followed by the priestess in charge of the candidates and several initiate priestesses of two seasons or more. The candidates followed them in twos, entered the dance enclosure, and were joined by a young drummer and two boys playing gongs to the beat of the drums.

Now the time had come for the initiates to perform for the first time as members of the society of the Language of the Drums.

Adeoha and her sisters danced through the compound, stopped and stood before the sacred trees and shrines, and commenced with songs, chants, and more dancing, thrilling the audience. Then, the candidates returned to the culthouse, followed by Ezogbo.

The moonrise added a colorful milieu or splendor to the festivities; the men and women filled the time enjoying food and drink while the children collectively played in the sand and amused themselves with sundry drawings of what they saw.

As the drum rhythms began, most activities came to a stop, and then the initiates emerged from the cult-house, completing the first phase of initiation. But it would be moons before the higher levels of instruction would be completed.

The final day of ceremonials began with no hint to the priestesses, or anyone else for that matter, of what the day would bring.

After arriving, the people noticed that the four appliques were now six and not positioned in a square as the previous day, but all in a straight line, hanging from high to the ground as one applique, one picture story.

The new appliques were about the "oracle," a forest full of the ancestral spirits seemingly in a celebratory mood, natures' spirits moving about, many houses and young people of all ages, and the Mami Wata spirits in a river nearby.

The spectators are in awe of the applique of the oracle, its craftsmanship, mastery, and elegance. All visitors can now view what has been discussed and imagined about the oracle for ages within the compound walls.

Twenty attendants illuminated the night holding torch-like, baobab branches in clay cups of palm oil.

Later, Ezogbo spoke to the initiates, "As you dance the rite of commemoration for the ancestors to thank them for preserving the prophecy of the oracle, remember that within these revered walls you may hold the key in times yet to come.

"Perhaps, one of you will come forward and feel the ancestor's energy within you and become one with the drumming flow; and perform the rite of anticipation. The ancestor's spoken word is in the drum language. You can communicate with them through your ritual, the dance patterns, and your energy.

Then the initiates returned to the cult-house, followed by Mama Ezogbo. A short time later, the initiates emerged from the cult-house after their initiation was completed. They were led to the dance enclosure by an elderly priestess on one side, five graduate priestesses on the other, and seated on mats.

Then, after a short interlude, each of the twelve stood and performed the dance of emergence. Then the dancers began to perform the ritual patterns of the dance of commemoration. The spectators sat in awe of the dancing, and cowries rained on the earth from the appreciative spectators.

Suddenly, Adeoha began to forge new complex patterns and rhythms into her dance. She could hear the drumbeats vibrating through her whole being. Her movements brought forth new energy, and the drummer began to alter the beats with jarring rhythms and dissonant patterns to match her power.

The attendants' spontaneity followed Adeoha and the drummer and the gong players on both sides. The cheers rose to an almost deafening high when Adeoha and the drummer appeared in a creative contest. But from this point on, some among the society's members recognized they were in the presence of something unique and different.

The priestesses and members of the group who had waited their entire lives to witness what they were seeing took a moment before they realized the dance of anticipation was upon them. Then, they began to interpret the poetic prophecy of when the oracle would set new rhythms of magical knowledge upon the world.

"We have on this occasion," the chief-priestess said, "seen the commemoration rites performed to its utmost by the initiates in homage to the ancestors. Then the girl [Adeoha] stepped into another realm, and her dance and the drum language beckon us to another time and place."

"I have been hoping to hear this drum language in my time," the elderly priestess said.

"I feel blessed to have been here," Chief Ezogbo said, "and to witness this occasion."

"We must not forget the role of the young drummer," one of the graduate priestesses was overheard to say.

"Surely, no initiation ceremony in memory has been so great as this," said a woman leaving the compound. And that sentiment and similar expressions would resound throughout Da's Belly in the coming days.

Three days later, Adeoha was visited by her first friend Sewextu at her house, and they commenced walking through the compound together, talking with each other and with friends.

"You dismiss what happened with your dance so easily," Sewextu said. "Will I see you at the compound?"

"I won't return; I have informed them," Adeoha said.

"I thought you might stay a little longer," Sewextu said.

"You of all people should know it. I am not the type for this occupation. None of it was my doing. It was only the strange set of events that placed me there."

*****

Two weeks passed, and Adeoha decided to visit Sewextu at the language drums compound.

"I'm surprised," Sewextu said, "we are not allowed, visitors. But because of your status as an initiate and what you have done for the society, it was permitted."

"I was greeted warmly by everyone," Adeoha said.

"We have missed you," Sewextu said.

"Let's go to the tree forest," Adeoha said, "and sit at the stream."

"I must remain here a little longer," Sewextu said, "We only made the first step; there is a higher order, where the verse is taught. In four or five moons, I will know all that I need. After that, I will either leave in the manner you have or complete the training."

"What will you do now, Adeoha?" Sewextu said.

"I want to trade in big places," Adeoha said. "I may have been reluctant to leave home and go out on my own, but I am ready now, and I'm going to make a move soon. I don't know in what way, but it will come to me; I can feel it."

"I have spoken with the priestesses," Sewextu said, "and told them of my plans. Now we are being instructed in verse the way we were with the dance. The verse compositions about the oracle are beautiful to behold."

"I know it was to become a verse master was your primary reason for seeking membership and remaining," Adeoha said.

"I feel there is much more I can do with our words, with our songs; the verse form is like the rhythmic patterns of the drum, with its rhythms and beats and measures," Sewextu said.

"Your heart understands much, Sewextu, Adeoha said "you are like the needleworker who sews the appliques about our stories and traditions, except you want to do these things with verse, much the same way Mama Ezogbo does with her calling when she travels.

"Yes," Sewextu said. I think it is why the language drums promise me so much leeway,

"I see you now, roaming through Da's Belly, the spearhead for the society, telling the oracle stories in song and verse and dance," Adeoha said and laughed.

"I will see you again soon," Sewextu said, and the two friends embraced and went their separate ways.

CHAPTER FOUR

A week later, Adeoha rose at sunrise, and after completing the language drums exercises, she prepared for the marketplace. But, before leaving, she entered the cook room where she found her mother, Lamtaala, and her little sister, Oshun.

Looking at the two of them together reminded Adeoha of when she was learning the things necessary to sell in the marketplace, a little salt, some sugar cakes, and sweetmeats, and she'd be off.

"Adeoha, guess what!" Oshun said.

"The start of your school days is near," Adeoha said.

"I can't wait to enter the bush and learn its secrets," Oshun said.

Oshun's words recalled in Adeoha a like time in the bush when she was Oshun's age, learning the magic of the aziza is not like the magic of Legba; it is a branch of magic where medicine comes from leaves and herbs. Hence, the secrets her sister was anxious to learn.

"I haven't heard mention of the household arts; that's part of your school days too," Lamtaala said.

"Mother, may I tell sister mine the things you said about her," Oshun said.

"Shhhh!" Lamtaala said. "Adeoha's head is filled enough."

"What have you been telling her, Mother?" Adeoha said. Oshun grinned with pride, knowing she was the center of the conversation.

"Mother says that of late, your manner has changed," but the words were hardly out of her mouth when Adeoha gave her a big hug and dashed out the door and ran across the compound.

Gaye and Tsawi, two of Tubutu's female slaves, awaited with her wares, and off to the marketplace, she went.

Today is Mioxi, the first day of the Dahomean four-day week, and each day is spiritually connected and a time when no Dahomean works in the field. So Adeoha looked forward to having a good time; everyone would be there, friends she hadn't seen since in three moons.

As Adeoha entered the market, she glanced at the mound of earth where the aiza was. She could have sworn the ax'iza or aiza, the spirit which protects the markets and many other places, gave her a mischievous wink. The thought came to her head the day might be different.

Adeoha's reason for coming was the chance to move about and socialize with the other women who come from many walks of life.

A line of trees at one corner of the market and a few poles strung together with thatched cloths were the only shelter from the glaring sun. By the early afternoon, Adeoha had sold her things. But instead of returning home, she told Gaye and Tsawi to find a place, and she would call them when she was ready to leave.

Adeoha spent the time talking with the women traders and the women who sold food at the market. But today, she listened intently as the women discussed the various obstacles encountered on the roads between Atogon, Akpe, and Allada. Although she heard these stories before, this time, they struck a chord in her. Then she spent time with the children teaching and playing games with them.

But something was different; the male buyers and sellers grabbed her thoughts as if she was doing business with them. It was not an easy task maneuvering her way through the rows of sellers and buyers while at the same time trying to avoid stepping on the mats or places the sellers displayed their articles.

Finally, she stopped, aroused by several men talking about a big four-day market at Tori, just north of Ouidah, where countless people come to buy and sell.

Next, she found herself at the far side of the market, alongside the smiths and weavers. All sorts of ideas found their way into her head. Then, for the first time, she carefully surveyed how they managed their businesses.

"I can do that," she murmured, "buy a hoe or knife here and sell it there."

She caught herself, surprised at her thoughts. She began to list the things she would have to do to trade in several markets. She marked each of the men's occupations and reckoned the articles they made and sold.

Adeoha, when ready to leave, found Gaye and Tsawi, and she placed a present on the earthen mound of the aiza as a thank you for the possible, new course in her life.

"Tomorrow, I will speak with Mother mine," Adeoha thought as she made her way home.

Later, Adeoha lay on her sleeping mat thinking about her time at the marketplace earlier that day and learning about the market at Tori and how it was like a Hevioso thunderbolt struck her, and from that came the plan to launch her new trading business.

Then she thought about how Sewextu, with a twist of her tongue, and her father's tradition, had fated her to the language drums.

"But now it's done," Adeoha thought, "now I can pursue my ambition to trade; nothing has changed for me, despite what has happened of late."

"I'm intelligent, and I live in a world of reality," she thought. "I can't bring myself to believe in all the spiritual forces of my culture, and the things I feel now, I can only lay the cause to my time within the language drums community.

As the dawn approached, Adeoha could hear Lamtaala stirring in another part of the house. Soon, they greeted each other and walked outside. "You seem to be in a cheerful way," Lamtaala said.

"I'll come right out and tell you, Mother," Adeoha said. "I would like to trade in the markets beyond Atogon."

"I'm sure that will come in time if that is what you truly want," Lamtaala said.

"I'm talking about now," Mother. "I will begin here, and when the market closes, I will go to Allada, and when the market closes there, I will go to Akpe, and from there to the big four-day market at Tori, and then back to Atogon.

Lamtaala looked at her daughter, "By Aido Hwedo, the sacred serpent who accompanied Mawou when she created the world," Lamtaala said, "from where did this idea spring?"

"I had this strange feeling during the end of my time at the language-drums, but it was not clear to me until yesterday at the market," Adeoha said. "The women who sell at the market in Atogon walk a day's journey to the markets at Allada and Akpe, where they buy what's needed and return. I can do more."

"I will listen." Lamtaala said as they continued walking.

"Thank you, Mother," Adeoha said.

"I will begin on Zogodu [Dahomean four-day week] because it is a favored by the gods to begin a journey such as mine, and after the market closes, I will go to Allada, and my band and I will enjoy the night and trade at Allada on Adjaxi.

"After that, I will trade in the market at Akpe on Mioxi, but instead of returning home, I go to Tori. Because it is a long, hard road, I will travel on Adokwi and reach Tori before the night has come and rest. Then, I will trade at Tori on Mioxi and Zogodu. After that, I will return to Atogon on Adjaxi."

"You have not been away from home unless in the company of your father or me or your brother. You have done little work at our market in Atogon," Lamtaala said.

"Did you not start your business at my age," Adeoha said.

"I was sixteen," Lamtaala said, "but I was older before I traveled the distance you are talking.

"Tori can bring me a great profit," Adeoha said, "because it is close to Ouidah, where the goods from across the sea arrive. And the traders bring the goods into the interior and set the prices. Can I not do the same?

"Tori can also be a dangerous place because of the slave coffle's going to Ouidah," Lamtaala said.

"I know I am capable of doing this," Adeoha said. "I have thought it out clearly."

"Suppose you do reach Tori without peril," Lamtaala said, "you do not possess the experience or the cunning to buy and sell among wily traders."

"I will manage, Mother," Adeoha said. "And hopefully, I have yours and my father's shrewdness in business."

"Now the question is," Lamtaala said, "who will follow you, and who will trust their goods to you?"

"I will find the people and things I need," Adeoha said, "it is my Fa, my destiny."

"I have not heard such strong talk from you before," Lamtaala said. And what about Lord Ewansi and the council. They will not think kindly of your absence if your travels take you from Dahomey during the planting.

"It is only for now," Adeoha said. "Once the rains come and planting begins, I will stop and fulfill my obligation to the land."

"It would not be as difficult," Lamtaala said, "if you were of your father's clan. However, my Father [Lord Ewansi] will see your venture (if anything happens to you) as a great risk to the marriage price he will command when you wed."

"I have considered that," Adeoha said. "Since I reached the age of fourteen, I am no longer counted with the pebbles of children in the Dahomean census."

It was Adeoha's way of saying she would start her business no matter the council's decision.

"With the pebbles from the census," Adeoha said, "the king knows the number of men, women, boys, and girls in all the districts of Dahomey. So the king can plan and mobilize for war at any time, and I can be constricted into a women's regiment of the army. If I'm at the age to fight for Dahomey, then I'm at the age to start a business anywhere in Da's Belly."

"You are headstrong like your father and filled with pride like an overflowing river," Lamtaala said.

"Does this mean you favor my suit," Adeoha said.

"Sometimes, the spirits of cause and effect can be most powerful," Adeoha replied. "Take the case of when your father asked for my hand in marriage. Lord Ewansi had bought a large plantation; though his workforce was large, it was not enough to bear the burden of the new land he bought, and he faced a great loss. So he devised a way to trick Tubutu and agreed to the betrothal, though he had no intention of going through with it."

"He called upon the Dahomean custom, Tubutu would shower his future father-in-law with gifts, and cultivate his new land,

and after the harvest, he would have a great profit and repay Tubutu the money he spent and end the betrothal, as custom allows."

"I know my grandfather; he has no sentiment," Adeoha said, "but you did wed. I can't imagine what happened to change his mind."

"Tubutu's wealth was not an exaggeration," Lamtaala said. "He showed up at my father's field with his dokpwe of one hundred men [a group of men in cooperative labor] and began clearing his fields for planting, roofing his houses, and digging new and deeper wells. He showered my mother [Lady Glyya] with cloths from across the sea, fine jewelry, and had his laborers take her goods to the marketplace and kept her cook fires aflame."

The story lit up both their faces with joy.

"Lord Ewansi had no choice but to approve the marriage," Lamtaala said, "for there was no way he could repay Tubutu for all the work he and his dokpwe did on his behalf."

"I'm glad you told me this story, Mother."

"I told you this because when you do a thing," Lamtaala said, " sometimes there can be certain forces pushing you that you are not aware of."

"I don't understand," Adeoha said.

"I was just saying," Lamtaala said, "this thing with the language drums, how you come to be there, what happened while you were there, now this plan of yours, and the sudden change in you."

"What are you saying, Mother," Adeoha said.

"Look at what you're planning now," Lamtaala said, "you use to scoff at other Dahomeans for doing the same thing."

"Yes, Mother," Adeoha said, "I should not have done so in the way that I did. Guezo is like a jacal howling in the wind, and we are his prey as we go about our work. The loud noise gets our attention as he tells us to work harder and harder and spend all our waking breath at our task because it is the only way we can be happy.

"Yet we are an industrious people, and hard work is our custom and our tradition. He says these things to keep our minds off the slave hunts and endless wars against defenseless people and leave us no time to express discontent at the injustice in our inner lives and the lives of our neighbors."

"I see you have not lost your willingness to express your political views," Lamtaala said.

"Are my words not true, Mother?" Adeoha said.

"That is not the point," Lamtaala said, "you are older now. Your words are no longer those of a child. Therefore, you must practice caution in Da's Belly. Have you not witnessed the fate of highborn Dahomeans who are politically troublesome."

*****

Two days passed, Adeoha, with her plan well in hand, walked in the starlight through the compound, stopping briefly to talk with Oshun and her half-brothers and half-sisters before going on to her father's house.

They embraced and sat outside his bungalow.

"Father mine, Adeoha said, speaking in the courtly Foy [Fon] language.

Tubutu eyed her curiously, suspecting she was up to something.

"Have I not acquired that Abomey, aristocratic accent, she said, "you pushed me to learn in my childhood."

"You and your brother O'Gwumike have done well, Tubutu said, "and Oshun follows a like path."

"Father mine," Adeoha said, "you have always shielded me from the not so pleasant side of life. You have kept me from Abomey, where King Guezo reigns. You have kept me from Whydah because of what goes on there."

Tubutu reached out and placed his huge hand on his daughter's shoulder.

"Next year, I will take you to both places," Tubutu said.

"I know your reason was good," Adeoha said, "and it was what you felt was best for me, but I am no longer a child."

"I did not feel that Ouidah was the place for you to see life," Tubutu said. "For you to see men and women driven like cattle, shackled and branded, that was for another time in your life." Tubutu shrugged his shoulders and sighed.

"Abomey is different, Father mine," Adeoha said.

"Abomey was more about keeping the eyes of the Leopard [King Guezo] and the princes from you," Tubutu said.

"The discourse we had during our last time together," Adeoha said, "has given me a new perspective of the world. So now I wish to seek out my own life, to experience the world with my eyes, to embrace the people of other places and hear their stories, and to know life in all its forms."

"You sound as if you plan to leave Atogon soon," Tubutu said.

Adeoha proceeded to have much the same conversation with Tubutu as she had with Lamtaala.

"As I told mother," Adeoha said, "I will ask the council's permission to journey from here to Allada, and from there to Akpe, but instead of returning to Atogon, I will travel to the great market at Tori."

"You have a good plan," Tubutu said. "But there are a lot of issues that come with so precise an undertaking."

"There's a road to Tori not traveled much," Adeoha said. "It's close by the road used by those in the king's employ, who haul goods from the sea coast at Ouidah to Abomey."

"So far," Tubutu said, your plan is possible."

"I think I can find the old road, Adeoha said. "

"The whole area, including the road you speak off, is filled with danger," Tubutu said. "You will make a good target for what you might carry.

"Can you ask the diviner or bokonon to throw the fa seeds on my behalf," Adeoha laughed and said.

"Yes," Tubutu said. "I'll ask Odugbe."

"That's a long road from Akpe to Tori; you'll have to gather your things and travel all day," Tubutu said. "And you must have strong people who are ready for war. And your return from Tori to Atagon will be no less hazardous."

"I will give my people a good night to rest and leave at sunrise and reach Tori before nightfall," Adeoha said. "The next day and the following day, I will trade at Tori. Then, after a night of rest, my people will be ready for the long road back to Atogon."

"The way you have it," Tubutu said, you will be gone from home five full days, and parts of two others, returning to Atogon late on the seventh day. That is a lot for one who has never been away from home on their own."

"I can do this, Father mine," Adeoha said.

"I will support you as best as I can," Tubutu said. "But keep in mind, the xenuga is head of the clan and has more power over a girl-child than anyone. But in both instances, this could be in your favor."

"How so," Adeoha asked curiously.

"If you want to buy and sell expensive goods," Tubutu said, which you will need to do to make a good profit, then you will need well-off Dahomeans. You will do well to court the xenuga and the other influential family heads into your buying circle."

"I can use this time to view some of the expensive articles from across the sea and how they are traded," Adeoha said. "It will help me in the big markets, but for now, I will look for items on demand that commoners can afford."

"Ajatauvi holds court over the council, and Ewansi is his kin who he favors," Tubutu said, "and Ewansi favors O'Gwumike like a son."

"I see Father mine," Adeoha said. But, I still have to get the people I need and a way to carry my load between markets."

"It will come down to how you and your people fair if trouble finds you," Tubutu said.

"Our talk has been good, Father mine, Adeoha said. "You have pushed me."

*****

The next day, Adeoha set out to see O'Gwumike, whose compound was an extension of Ewansi's. He was not at home, but his men-servants told her he was away on business at Tendji and Abomey.

Three days later, O'Gwumike sent Adeoha a message by his man-servant that he had returned.

O'Gwumike is nineteen years old and stands six foot four inches tall. He is often compared to the Ashantis'Ganu nlan royal hunters. He is four years older than Adeoha, so they were close enough in age to form a strong bond growing up. Adeoha relied on the respect he had always given her.

"Greetings," Adeoha said, "male child of the same father and mother," and O'Gwumike responded in kind, and they embraced.

"What mischief have you involved yourself in now, and how can I help," he said as they entered his workshop.

"Before I tell the reason I am her, O'Gwumike," Adeoha said. "May I ask you how you fared on your travels to Abomey and Tendji."

"My time in Abomey was given to the crafts and good times with friends," O'Gwumike said. "I went to Tendji to sell two of my calabashes to the head of an Ayato clan, ascribing the deeds of the tohwiyo [founder] of his clan."

"Your name is rising among the young nobles and upper class because of your carved calabash, drawing attention to me as well," Adeoha said.

"Thank you, Sister mine, O'Gwumike said. "Now, let me know your reason for this visit."

"I ask for your support in my new business," Adeoha said.

"Tell me more," O'Gwumike said,

Adeoha repeated the main points of her conversations with Lamtaala and Tubutu."

Of course, I support you," he said, "and I will give you one of my calabashes to take with you, for it may attract eyes to your business at Tori, hungry to feast on the art of Dahomey."

"Thank you," Adeoha said. "It will be of great help."

"I will reach out to Ewansi for the purpose you have stated," O'Gwumike said. "Mind you, this is not an easy thing you seek to do, and I would have hesitated, not wanting to put you in harm's way, were it not for your time with the language drums."

"Yes," Adeoha said, "my time with them seems to have brought some change to my life."

"You did not have thoughts like this before your time with the language drums," O'Gwumike said.

Adeoha smiled at his words while thinking, the people close to her see a change in her, but they attribute it to the language drums society and not her own head, but that was okay.

"And because you participated in the war games of the Ahosi," O'Gwumike said, "you learned to handle the musket, machete, and the club with no equal, male or female. So anyone on the road who sees you as easy prey will soon discover the lioness in you."

Adeoha listened to O'Gwumike's words with fervor, and then her thoughts slowly drifted in tune with the enchantment of the carved calabashes in his workshop.

"I am amazed at the insight you bring into making your calabashes," Adeoha said. "The meaning of the symbols and proverbs are miracles of your art and tell many stories of love that touch the depth and the height of human emotion.

"I have felt the joy of the recipient when a calabash is received from a loved one, and the appreciation it gives the sender when seeing his words of love become imagery of nature and life caressing the heart of a loved one."

Adeoha remembered when she received a calabash with a gift inside from an ardent admirer. The carver did not possess the skill of O'Gwumike, but it would not have mattered. She returned it and the gift inside—to do otherwise would have meant acceptance to the sender.

"Just hard work and a lot of studying," O'Gwumike said.

"Yes," Adeoha said, "you have done well since your carefree days with your friend gorging yourself with millet beer like an elephant at the stream."

"Yes," O'Gwumike said, "my friends and I had many good times together."

"Your art is fit for a king," Adeoha said, "and only a king could afford it," and they both laughed.

"On a more serious note," Adeoha remarked, you could be seen as politically troublesome to the King and his counselors if the injustices you hint at in some of your calabashes were not cloaked in proverbs and riddles."

"I guess I was looking for a way to use my art for good," O'Gwumike said. "I was thinking about how I could bring in an apprentice from outside the family; that's how it started. I made a few calabashes for some commoners I know."

"Your idea of an apprentice is a good one," Adeoha said. "It won't sit well with the family guild, but you can make it work."

"Though the serpent does not eat millet, he will eat it when in the stomach of a rat," a fitting proverb, O'Gwumike said to Adeoha.**

It was then that Adeoha saw a calabash different from the rest.

"Tell me about this one," Adeoha said.

"It's something I started on my own," O'Gwumike said.

"The design seems to encircle a bird and a fish, and the rest of it I can't tell," Adeoha said.

"It's a girl at the seaside filling her calabashes with water from the sea," O'Gwumike said. "A passerby asks her what she was doing. She tells him she's going to empty all the sea into her calabashes. The passerby tells her it was impossible to empty the entire sea into her calabashes no matter how many she had."

Adeoha stood there looking at her brother, waiting to hear the point of the story.

"Mawou-Lissa is like the great sea, O'Gwumike said, "and our minds are like a calabash; they have not the capacity for to knowledge of the Creator, as some men profess. I think if we stood before Mawou, she would slap our faces for our audacity."

Adeoha listened silently; it was apparent that he wanted to leave his thoughts from his mind and profess them to somebody in the real world because what sounds good to the head may not sound good in a world of reality.

"I see myself not unlike the diviner or sorcerer," O'Gwumike said. I also tell men what they want to hear, based on my knowledge of the past. So I take liberty with the sayings of the proverbs and when I interpret the words of Mawou."

**Proverb translated from Dahomey: An Ancient West African Kingdom: Melville J. and Francis S. Herskovits

"They both are honorable professions," Adeoha said. "And what you do is fine and noble."

"I have good feelings for you, Sister mine," O'Gwumike said.

"We have grown tall together," Adeoha said, and the two embraced heartily, and she headed for home.

As Adeoha skipped merrily along, an idea came to her head from Tubutu's calabash story.

"I don't have to fill calabashes with an ocean, only a few large storage pots to transport my goods between markets," she thought.

The rainy season was approaching, and Adeoha was anxious to embark on her new adventure. All had gone well, O'Gwumike had pushed Ewansi, and in turn, Ewansi moved Ajatauvi, and the venerable elders approved her new business.

Now on this day, Adeoha lay beside the palm groves that she would inherit. She had need to see Sewextu, yet she didn't want to return to the language-drums so soon or disturb Sewextu from her training. But she had no choice.

Adeoha's meeting before the priestesses and priests at the language drums went well after telling them the nature of her new business and the travels it entailed, and why she needed Sewextu to come with her to Ajajou.

Adeoha walked into the courtyard, and her eyes fell upon Sewextu sitting in the shade of a palm tree

"You seem to be very much into what you were doing," Adeoha said."

"I was rehearsing in my mind some of the verse sequences I have learned," Sewextu said, "and composing a new song.

"I've come to take you home," Adeoha said and smiled. Then she explained why she had come.

"I'll start gathering my things," Sewextu said.

"The society as yet hasn't rendered their decision," Adeoha said.

"It won't matter," Sewextu said, "it's my duty as your first friend."

Adeoha and Sewextu made their way to Ajajou, and after much discussion, the potters would make four specially designed large vessels for her new business.

While she was home, Sewextu decided to give a performance, which surprised her family and a small gathering of friends, evoking time and setting with a new song, which led to her family tree's verse sequence.

Next, Adeoha had to find the women she needed. The first person that came to her head was Isaige. She was middle height and thick—and a terror to behold if crossed.

Isaige liked Adeoha as soon as they met, hearing of her tenacity in the Ahosi games [female soldiers of the Dahomean army]. She was also a noble from a distinguished family. She pointed out to Adeoha four women tough enough to take on the journey, and Adeoha chose Gaye and Tsawi, making them a band of eight.

If they had to stand and fight, only Adeoha and Isaige were to shoot. The rest were to load and pass the muskets. Next, with the anya rods and rope to secure the four storage vessels, two in the band can carry two storage vessels, two take the other two, and two will alternate at intervals, while Adeoha or Isaigye or both keep vigil.

Adeoha secured six muskets, including her assegai sword given by Tubutu, and Isaigye brought her own bush knives and clubs. Finally, she gave an offering to her head—her intelligence—as well as the Vodun and ancestors. Now, she is ready to walk a new road, for the day after tomorrow is Zogodu.

The next day, there were a few things she had to do. The last was to visit the yovos and Mautusan. So, from her father's compound, she headed for the compound of Mautusan, where the sounou gnonou ayounwewenon [white man and white woman] lived under his protection.

CHAPTER FIVE

As Adeoha walked along the road to Mautusan's compound, she was taken back when Robert naïve [Mister Robert] and Patricia viovi [Lady Patricia] first come to Atogon with Mautusan.

Adeoha found Patricia with the women and children at a stream nearby Mautusan's compound.

"I don't have much time; I leave in two days," Adeoha said.

"So soon," Patricia said. "How long will you be away this time."

"By your time, a week and one day," Adeoha said.

"I will have to learn, again, to get along without you," Patricia said.

"It will be for a short time," Adeoha said. "I want to continue to speak your language and learn this thing you call algebra."

"And I as well look to continue to learn from you," Patricia said. "There is still much to teach me about Dahomey.

"Maybe, I can bring more to our discourse," Adeoha said, "the road I travel will take me other places in Dahomey, and I will come upon new people and learn their lives."

"You have intended to trade in a far-off land for as long as I have known you," Patricia said. "

"The places I go now are not so distant," Adeoha said, "but it's good to walk this crossroad in my life."

"Are naïve Robert and Mautusan about." Adeoha asked.

"Robert is with the men clearing the fields. He can't wait for the planting to begin," Patricia said. "Farming and the soil are in his blood. Now that he has his own fields to cultivate and harvest, it has given purpose to his life and many good friends among his dokpwe.

"There's a glow in your eyes," talking about these things," Adeoha said.

"Robert and I had little to do when we first came to Atogon," Patricia said. "I thought I would be able to teach, but it was not to be because of the King's edict that we shall be invisible while in Dahomey."

"You have both managed well under trying circumstances," Adeoha said. "The villagers like you, and the women see you as one of them."

"I owe much of it to you," Patricia said. For three years, we have found secret places in the bush, there I have been able to satisfy my want for teaching through you, and it has brought me joy seeing how fast you have mastered each subject."

"The things I have learned from you will serve me well one day," Adeoha said. "The traders I meet along the road will say, '"who is this sapling, who can read and write the language of the whites, and know their algebra and geometry.'"

"As far as my acceptance by the villagers," Patricia said, "that is because you are nobility, and once they saw that we are friends . . . "

"My status may have been of help at first," Adeoha said, but they have come to like you and Robert naïve because of what they see in you."

"It might not have turned out that way," Patricia said, "if you did not spend so much time teaching me to speak your language and the gestures and nuances associated with it."

"We have learned much from each other," Adeoha said, "as it should be among friends."

"I will never forget the time you told me you had something to show me," Patricia said. So we went deep, deeper into the bush, where we came upon the habitat of an elephant herd, and I learned when we followed them, they are the most beautiful, compassionate creatures on this green earth."

"The one you call Obi, the matriarch of the family. It was both sad and heartfelt to see," Patricia said, "when she came upon a dead elephant whom she recognized as her child, and how the other elephants ran to her and caressed her in such a caring and loving way."

"I went with my parents to see an elephant at an exhibition. I couldn't have been more than one or two at the time, so I don't remember it, but I remember they told me how cruel it was to keep such a magnificent animal captive in a circus and subjected to abuse, just to perform a few tricks.

"Your parents are wise,' Adeoha said. "The self-existent spirit has created all the animals of the world, and that alone speaks well on their behalf."

The two of them waved to everyone and went down the road in the setting sun's light towards Mautusan's compound.

Upon seeing each other, Adeoha and Robert embraced fervently. Then, Patricia explained all that Adeoha had told her about putting her band together and the things needed to leave Dahomey.

"You have accomplished a lot in a short time," Robert said. "I wish you a good road.

"One does what is necessary," Adeoha said.

"Adeoha and I were talking earlier about our early days here," Patricia said, and how you acquired land."

"When we first came to Atogon, Robert said, I followed the men of the village into the forest looking to gather rocks and soil, anything to take back home to raise my status.

"By the end of our first year in Dahomey, which coincided with the end of the short planting season. Mautusan saw how interested I was in farming, and he suggested I acquire land, but in doing so, I would have to go through all the same rituals and ceremonials as a Dahomean would. It helped endear me to the people because every Dahomean, regardless of occupation, practices cultivation.

"I learned from Mautusan before I could clear the field for planting, I would have to give him a sample of the soil, for his diviner [the bokono who interprets Fate, Destiny], and then hold my breath. As Mautusan mentioned, there were other things I had to do before I could begin, based on Dahomean custom and culture, but all turned out well."

"I'm amazed by the way you have maneuvered your way through a culture as complex as ours [Fon]," Adeoha said.

"I was astonished," Robert said, "when my dokpwe told me that for my second season, it would not be good to plant the millet in the same field as last season. And where I grew peanuts my first season, I would do well to plant maize my second season or plant the maize and yams together because their roots nourish each other, and from this, my second harvest was exceptional."

"The land Robert acquired," Patricia said, "changed my life too and brought us closer together—and Robert and Patricia inched closer together and held hands. I began taking care of our fields and taking charge of the harvest with the help of the women of our household."

"Your household is small," Adeoha laughed and said, "you made a good profit in selling what was left over."

"I was hoping to see Mautusan," Adeoha said, "do you expect him soon?"

"We've grown accustomed to seeing Mautusan disappear from time to time, sometimes two or three Dahomean weeks, says he's going into the bush to hunt, and for other things," Robert said. "He takes either Tehseloh or Gbwe with him."

"Let me leave you now," Adeoha said, "I have much to think about," and she embraced the yovos and left there.

Adeoha skipped along the road, not a care in the world, for tomorrow was a day she had envisioned for a long time. But, as she began thinking about it, her head kept going back to Mautusan and Robert naive and Patricia viovi.

116

She recalled the times Mautusan had come to her school. He would tell the most fantastic stories of his travels and the people he encountered along the way.

Adeoha's favorite was the tale of how he and his little band of eight—himself, the yovo couple, his two retainers, and three crewmen from the region whence they came. They traveled by sea, river, and land for almost two and a half moons, crossing the Kong, the Fante, and the Akan countries before reaching Dahomey.

"If it were not for Mautusan's visits to my school," Adeoha thought, "I would not have come to know the yovo couple in the manner that I have."

Adeoha smiled as she recalled their first meeting. She had come to the marketplace with her first friend Sewextu and her third friend Nneonee. The strangers with Mautusan were dark from the sun and not unpleasant to the eyes. Mautusan seemed to look at her, and his voice was drum-spoken and echoed above the loud noise of the crowd. "Will one of you come forth and be a friend to this man and woman."

Adeoha stepped forward, moved by Mautusan's roaring voice and the man's and woman's demeanor. She stood before the woman and extended both her hands in friendship. Then she opened both her hands in the same fashion to the man.

They say the earth is Mawou's kingdom, including the yovo lands across the great water, Adeoha thought. The way the yovo couple's and Mautusan's roads crossed and how they came to Atogon leaves me with much to ponder.

Most of it I have heard from Patricia viovi and Robert naïve, and the rest of it through Mautusan. Mautusan says his Fa, Destiny brought him to Dahomey, but Lady Patricia and Mister Robert provoked it. They must have a strong trust in each other, for they have put their lives in each other's hands.

*****

Patricia Warren and Robert Wringle were born during the last days of the War of 1812. They grew up about one hundred miles from each other. Patricia in Washington City, where her father worked at the Washington Navy Yard, and Robert in Henrico, Virginia, where his father was a planter.

During Robert's and Patricia's early school years, white Americans started creating colonization societies to resettle freed slaves and free people of color on the Afrikan continent of their ancestors.

Patricia felt that since the colony movement never got the support of free colored American's or freed slaves, it was not a practical solution. And Robert knew that those in bondage were the heart and soul of plantation life. Therefore, Southern planters were not about to permit their best-skilled workers, carpenters, masons, blacksmiths, and the like to leave their control and go to Afrika.

One day on a whim, Robert attended a lecture given by a noted geologist passing through town, and he became fascinated with the subject. The lecturer, seeing his interest, gave Robert a book on the natural sciences; the lecturer and the book opened him up to a new world.

As time passed, Robert's primary focus was on expanding his professional horizons as a geologist. Robert traveled to Philadelphia at the invitation of a friend to take in some lectures by well-known geologists at the Academy of Natural Sciences.

Patricia's focus was on higher education for women. She grew up when most Americans believed that young women did not need more education. However, she attended the Troy Female Seminary** and studied science, mathematics, and philosophy.

Patricia traveled from her home in Washington City to attend the formation of the American Anti-Slavery Society. There would be many female abolitionists attending she could talk with about adding women's higher education to the abolitionist cause.

As fate would have it, instead of going home after the men's convention, she added twelve more days to her stay when she learned the women were forming the Female Anti-Slavery Society of Philadelphia.

During this time, among its founding members and leaders, what surprised her, were prominent free black women—who also operated and taught educational and activism programs in their communities.

*****

"The things these women teach are not so different from the things I have learned from you," Adeoha said. "I would like to know about the women."

"Their story is for another day, Patricia said. They are a lot like the women of Lamtaala's gybe or social club. But I will say this, while I was in their company during the days leading up to the women's convention, we talked about various social issues, and Afrika came up.

It followed that some of the women expressed an interest in visiting Afrika, so Afrika was on their mind, but it was not on mine. If anything, I was thinking about visiting Paris, France; it's ironic, I'm the one who would come to Afrika."

**Founded by Emma Willard, the Troy Female Seminary opened in September 1821 for boarding and day students. The first school in the United States to offer higher education for women.

A strange place this Amerika, Adeoha thought. The whites and blacks come together and look to end human bondage. The whites appeal to the consciousness of their citizenry and call upon the sacred words of their ancestors.

Robert and Patricia met aboard the boat returning home. About a year later, after Robert's many visits to court Patricia, they were married and settled in Washington City—America's national capital.

*****

As the Wringle's sat at home one evening, Robert told Patricia about a position for a geologist in West Afrika by the Maryland Colonization Society.

"They're looking for someone to survey the Cape Palmas region," Robert said.

"Are you going to apply," Patricia said.

"The Society is probably looking for someone with more experience," Robert said.

Although Robert had little experience beyond his time as a surveyor's assistant, the members of the Society were so impressed with his time at the Academy of Natural Sciences, they moved his application through channels and summarily offered him the position.

Robert returned home with the good news. "What a stroke of good luck," Patricia said.

"I have to be able to leave right away," Robert said, "because they have a vessel leaving the port at Baltimore for Afrika any day now."

"How long will we be gone?" Patricia said, bringing a smile to Robert's face.

"I told them at the Society my wife would have to come with me," Robert said, "and they agreed. But I didn't want to assume you would want to come before asking you."

"How long will we be gone?" Patricia said.

"My contract with the Society is for one year," Robert said. "Add four months for travel; we should be back home in less than a year and a half."

As unlikely as it would seem, the way they would meet and marry, now they were going off to Afrika together.

On the fourteenth day of August 1835, Robert and Patricia Wringle boarded the Brig Daphne to their families and friends' dismay and departed the Port of Baltimore for the Grain Coast in West Afrika. The Daphne made a brief stop at Cape Mesurado, home to the American Colonization Society, and on the seventh day of November, came to the point of her final destination, Cape Palmas.**

The brig anchored in the open sea about three miles from shore because of the dangerous shallows; their landing onshore was carried out by the light and ingeniously crafted canoes of the natives. The ship's captain, Robert, and Patricia were escorted by staff to the agency house with surprising applause. Several representatives of the Society greeted them, and a man of the clergy and his wife who were recently married.

The young couple amazed Robert and Patricia; both had grown up on large plantations in South Carolina and Georgia. Reverend Wheeler and his wife tried in vain to have Robert and Patricia call them by their given names, Lawrence and Elizabeth, but they had too much respect for them.

**Cape Palmas and the Mena, or Kroomen, Francis Bacon: The Journal of the Royal Geographic Society of London Vol. 12 (1842).

Reverend Wheeler carried on many arduous tasks while battling the diseases of the climate. He looked to have his mission school up and running to teach some Grebo people English and then use them as teachers to help their brethren read and write a Grebo alphabet he was developing.

Robert Wringle began his geologic research along the coast; twenty-five miles west, twenty-five miles east, and thirty miles into the interior.

The Wringle's accommodations were about twelve miles inward from the coast in

White Town. It was not a great distance from Native Town. The Mena people spoke a dialect of the Grebo language, and the advanced students were learning English at the mission school. Robert and Patricia began to learn bits and pieces of their language, and within a few months, they were able to converse with the natives very well.

Robert and Patricia began to form a bond of friendship with the Grebo and found them industrious, intelligent, and characterized by patience and a sense of duty. But they felt the spirit of this place was ebbing, as the native tribes resisted foreign rule over them and their lands, and in this corner of Afrika, the settlers were a class above the natives and treated them as such.

Robert wanted to go into the interior beyond the lands of the coastal tribes and the agency's thirty-mile limit. His excursions into the interior the land elevated, and hills of no great height appeared.

From atop one of these hills, looking northeast, he could see high, blue peaks towering on the horizon. But to reach it would take traversing dangerous and unexplored land. So when he asked who could best guide him there and back, the one name he kept hearing on everyone's breath—Mautusan.

After the Wringle's first meeting with Mautusan, they concluded that he was amiable enough—despite his uncertain reputation. He was dark in color and about six feet tall and about fifty or so in age, but he moved like a twenty-year-old. He was known as a trader and merchant and often went on mysterious voyages. How he obtained his vast wealth was a matter of speculation, depending on the teller.

Robert, Patricia, and Mautusan managed to find time from their busy routines to sit and talk on several occasions, and Mautusan began to feel an immense liking for them. The months passed quickly, and Robert continued to push Mautusan to guide him into the interior and beyond the society's self-imposed limit.

One night, when the three of them were sitting on the beach talking, Robert posed the question again to Mautusan about guiding him into the interior.

"I would sooner journey with you across the countries of the Fante and Asante and the Akan," Mautusan said, "than take you into that part of the interior you speak of."

It was a harmless statement by Mautusan meant in jest and taken as such by Robert and Patricia, and they laughed heartily.

"Will you return to your country one day?" Patricia asked.

"I have been within a short distance many times by land and less by longboat," Mautusan said, "when I have turned away."

"Robert and I will be leaving Cape Palmas and going home soon," Patricia said.

"I wish I could return to my home as surely as you return to yours," Mautusan said.

"Is it a great distance from here," Robert said.

"Perhaps a month's journey or less, depending on the moon and tides and wind," Mautusan said.

"So Dahomey is the name of your country," Robert said, and Mautusan nodded his head.

After that time, Mautusan talked more openly about his life and family and growing up in Dahomey. Then, on one occasion, he told a story that Robert and Patricia could see moved him greatly, and he went deep into the night with it.

The Wringle's listened open-mouthed, which engendered in them reflections of their distant homes, and they emptied a flask of good brandy and saluted the crescent moon sky.

Mautusan began to smile as he spoke of his boyhood days at the seashore in Ouidah. "Besides my Foy [Fon] language and that of Ewe, I learned to speak the Portuguese, French, and English languages well from my father and grandfather. I often accompanied them when they had business at the European forts. My linguistic ability soon provided me with a good livelihood and a respected profession.

"The king [Angonglo] was assassinated, leaving his son [Adandozan] as ruler, ending my carefree and blissful life. He punished everyone he suspected. My father included, and my mother and my siblings were sent into slavery to Bahia. Then, under direct orders of the king, the Yovoga [viceroy of Ouidah] set a trap for my capture. But Legba did not take my breath, and I escaped with my head intact."

"We are saddened by what you have told us."

"No need, my friends, Mautusan said. "It happened long ago, and many good things have happened since. "I will share a little of it with you now, as I prefer to leave you with good thoughts."

*****

"Seven years after my escape, at a native festival, I met a ship captain called Dinocencio. He had chosen to live out his remaining days sailing the same waters he had sailed his entire life rather than return to the land of his birth, Portugal, Mautusan said.

"Dinocencio's father and grandfather had been mariners in the waters from the Grain Coast and Ivory Coast to the Bight of Benin and Niger. He still commanded his seventy-four-ton schooner and sometimes took on small cargoes.

"I spoke his language surprised him. He took me under his wings and brought me to Cape Palmas. He told me he would enjoy training a young sprout like me—it would add some spice and adventure to his remaining years.

"Dinocencio explained to me, because of Cape Palmas' position at the bend of the continent and the ocean's sharp change, it could one day become a major port of trade.

"'It is customary for European and American vessels to come to this region six or seven times a year, not counting the brigs on their way to the Bight of Benin and Niger, Dinocencio said. They must stop somewhere in this region to supply themselves with Kroomen, Fishmen—as the Europeans call the Mena—and get rice for their sustenance as little can be found leeward.

'"The slave traders come to this region for the same reason, and the European and American manufacturers make it a stop for selling and exchange by those who wish to go into the interior or sail further east.

'"Of course, there were no whites or settlements then. But when the Caucasians—Dinocencio called the whites by that name—and the colored American settlers came with the first colony, it was just the beginning, and more would follow, and spoil the native lands.'"

"Dinocencio was proven to be right in his thinking," Mautusan said. "Several colonies have been established since he joined his ancestors. Each one a step closer to Cape Palmas, and two years ago, the Maryland colony came to Cape Palmas, which brought you here."

"You must have thought a lot of him," Patricia said. "I can hear it in your voice when you speak of him."

"Yes!" Mautusan said. "My journey lead me down a good road, where my path and Dinocencio's crossed. Praise to Mawou Lissa."

"He seems to have been a special person," Robert said.

"That he was, Mautusan said, within a few years, true to his word, we prospered in the region of Cape Palmas. I learned about sailing and navigation from him—at least enough to help during our voyages.

"As time passed, Dinocencio started sailing his schooner, with me at his side, beyond the Grain Coast, and into the Ivory Coast and Gold Coast, and then the Bight of Benin, close to my home.

"Perhaps it was his way of repaying me for what he felt I had brought to his life. He had said to me often enough, in so many words, he did not want to see me make the same mistake that he had in not returning to his home in Portugal, at least on occasion, to visit his family and friends.

"I believe it was more than sentiment on Dinocencio's part. I think he felt there was a lot more he could teach me. Our business grew strong at the ports in the Bight of Benin, except Ouidah, where I could not conduct business out of respect for my family and friends sent into slavery from there. The ports at Popo and Porto Novo and Onim and Badagry kept me busy enough besides.

"The king's status must be growing strong with the Portuguese king; I said to Dinocencio one day as we watched a Portuguese ship set out from Ouidah. They honor the king by taking his representatives to Bahia."

"'Sometimes those things we take for granted can blind us to its true nature,'" Dinocencio said. "'It can be profitable to know what the King of Portugal and the

King of Dahomey talk about in their letters.'"

"I never thought about it, Mautusan admitted, because it concerned the human beings sent into slavery and the goods the Dahomean kings received in payment."

'"It is knowledge of these things that can make for us a good profit, Dinocencio said. For one thing, money is not as lively as in earlier days. I know that must appear so to the king of Dahomey, and the Regency of Portugal does not hold the king on high as they once did.'"

"Then things are not as they seem," Mautusan said.

'"Quite the contrary, Dinocencio said. This king and his father were anxious to learn about the wars between the European nations because they badly affected the trade of living beings at Ouidah.

'"It started harmlessly enough with the uprisings in Haiti and France. Then the French wars and the English abolished slavery and ran around pushing the other nations to do the same.

'"Closer to home, Bonaparte and the French army had my country on the run to Bahia. Now the Portuguese king and court are at Rio de Janeiro. The king's ambassadors are no longer received at the Royal Court. These events added insult to King Adandozan.

'"But for our business, the cost of textiles and other articles have begun to rise and fall with wide fluctuation. Sizeable profits are there for the taking if one is wise about the cargo of the Brazilian vessels and knows the correspondence between the Portuguese crown and the Dahomean king.'"

"So that's why you insisted I learn to read and write the words of the Europeans," Mautusan said. "Still, how can one see the words in their letters?"**

'"The Dahomean kings do not know how to read and write, but they have sent several embassies to Brazil, Dinocencio said. The first was in 1750, under King Tegbesu. So they have entrusted their words to an interpreter, but the interpreter has a memory of the words he wrote, and that is all we ask—a few memories for a few cowries.

'"It was from one of these letters, a few years back, that I learned it would be wise to buy a thousand rolls of tobacco, which I sold at a good profit.

**Dahomey, Portugal and Bahia: King Adandozan and the Atlantic Slave Trade: Ana Lucia Araujo: Howard University

'"There has always been palm wine and millet beer in Dahomey. But the European nations have found ways to compensate for the decline in the slave trade by pushing new exotic liqueurs and different kinds of wines and brandy, not only for the elite but also for the masses. European cloth is always in high demand. There are various ways to profit when I am no longer with you, and you have only to look around you.'"

"Dinocencio soon crossed the river and joined his ancestors, Mautusan said. "But I

138

soon came upon a way to take advantage of his last words."

"I was taken deep into the forest by a Krooman who was a member of my household. I went there to talk with the men who had made a big canoe I had recently seen. It could carry more bulk than a ship's longboat.

"I immediately employed the men and came away with four longboats, each one from the trunk of a different tree and ingeniously crafted by the native Mena people.

"I soon left Cape Palmas with my longboats and twenty Kroomen on a long voyage to Dahomey, stopping to buy and sell at the ports of entry along the way while picking up information to set prices at the ports ahead. We remained hidden by sailing the inlets where the rivers and streams found the sea through the skill of the Kroomen in my service.

"My success grew many times over, and I sent more Kroomen to work for me and built bigger and stronger longboats.

"My thoughts are of Dinocencio and the path he put me on. I began to send more Kroomen into my service and build safehouses inland at strategic locations between Palmas and Lagos

"The Kroomen are found on every vessel from the Gambia to Niger, providing me with information to move goods up and down the seacoast based on demand."

Robert and Patricia talked over what Mautusan had told them, convinced that remaining in Afrika was more than just an idle thought.

Two days passed, and on the third day, Robert and Patricia went to see Mautusan and found him outside his bungalow.

"Hello, my friends," Mautusan said.

"We would like to remain in Afrika for now," Robert said.

"We talked it over," Patricia said.

"I know you are not wanting to leave," Mautusan said.

"My job here has ended. We are to leave on the next ship to America," Robert said.

"From our conversations, we feel you have a longing for the land of your birth," Patricia said.

"I recall what you told us about your friend and mentor, Dinocencio, and his regret that he did not return home," Robert said, "then why not lift that burden from you now? And if you decide to return to your country, we would like to come with you."

"Well said, Mautusan said, "I will put your words in my thoughts." And Robert and Patricia left there.

No sooner than the yovos left, Mautusan thoughts were: his words to his friends were nothing more than good manners. There was no compelling reason to risk his neck by returning to Dahomey.

The Wringle's were pleased by what they had said to Mautusan. They had complete confidence in his ability to keep them from harm. If things did not turn out as planned, his access to American ships could get them passage to home, and by his telling, he had the men and arms for any contingency that may arise.

That very night of the same day, Mautusan fell into a deep sleep, but from rest came a dream that he couldn't remember when he awoke.

He stepped out of his bungalow into the sunrise and saw a bird flying high, and it flew down close and circled over him several times. The moment caused him to remember his dream.

The bird Wututu, the messenger of Sogbo, the sky vodun, sang to Mautusan in his dream. Then Wututu spoke: Sogbo tells you that his brother Legba bids you go to Dahomey with the yovos, which will cast suspicion from your true purpose, to make great riches.

Mautusan was not keen on magic, the mystical, and all the other spiritual staples of his culture. If anything, he chalked it up as a revelation of his intelligence.

Mautusan's decided he would return to Dahomey in the guise of a person of moderate wealth, whose principal income came from farming—but not enough wealth to interest the king, but strong enough to keep the tax collectors happy when reported to the Guezo. It would be business as usual once his plan was in effect, except he would run his business from inside Dahomey, right under the king's nose.

Mautusan considered the second phase of his plan: the police of Dahomey watch everyone coming and going, whites and blacks, near Ouidah, because the Yovoga must control the corridors to the beach, even the white men who want to conduct business on their ships must have special passes.

But Mautusan knew that one might travel east and west in the country without asking permission, though they watch you, they can't see in the darkness of night or the bush.

Mautusan felt that he could set out afoot, reach his men stationed at Little Popo, and head out to open sea beyond the eyes at

Ouidah and come ashore at Porto Novo, or Agado, or at Onim or Badagry, and even venture to the rich country of Benin.

On the third day after their talk, Mautusan went to see Robert and Patricia at their home in White Town.

"I'm going home, " Mautusan said. "If things go well, I may be there for some time, perhaps a year or two."

Mautusan believed that the mention of two years would dispel the young couple's notion of coming with him.

Speaking as one, Robert and Patricia said. "We still want to go with you. We're prepared to stay a year or even two."

"Then it is settled," Mautusan said. "I will not fight the vodun and my head. It seems to be your Destiny, as it is mine. So we shall go to Da's Belly together. You are my gbo, my magic charm, as I am yours."

"It goes without saying," Mautusan said, two whites will not be invisible long in Da's Belly. I will have to go before the Royal

Court and petition the king for your protection—and mine."

"Robert and Patricia were already in a state of high spirits about remaining in Afrika as they were, while not caring to acknowledge what could lie in wait.

The Wringle's told know one of their plan except for Reverend Wheeler and his wife. "You should consider waiting until the ship arrives," Reverend Wheeler said. "It should be soon if they're on schedule, and deliver your letters for your families to the captain, personally. It will put the onus on the captain rather than some third party you will never know."

"If we wait for the ship," Robert said, "Mautusan may change his mind."

"Mautusan seems reliable enough," Reverend Wheeler said, "and if he is intent on taking you to Dahomey with him, a few more days won't matter. "

Robert and Patricia waited, and they were glad for it, as they entrusted the letters to their families directly to the ship's captain.

As Mautusan and his group passed the great kingdoms on the way to Dahomey, he no longer despised the Leopard kings so much, for they were not alone in the trade of human beings.

Life had been relatively peaceful until the whites came from across the sea. Now, every powerful chief and every powerful country seem eager to jump into the slave trade. Sadly, it's the way of the world, for even the whites, before they took to it— lived in slavery in great numbers, according to Dinocencio.

Once they reached Glidji, Mautusan would go forward on his own, resting the young whites with his people and telling Tehselou and Gbwe what they must do if all did not go well: they should return to Cape Palmas with Robert and Patricia.

So Mautusan traveled north through the marshes and the home of the independent Popoe** people. He had developed a pact of friendship with them during his early years. Once he was beyond the waters of Aheme,

146

he was close to Allada, where he hoped to find the gbonuga of Allada.

Mautusan entered the compound. He continued to walk as it brought back long ago times when he romped and played like the children before him now.

The house servant told him Lord Awissou was at home and would see him, and Mautusan breathed a sigh of relief, for that might not have been the case because a chief's duties require him to travel often throughout the various districts of the province on the king's business. Moreover, they were not age-mates, and many years had passed, and he hoped Awissou remembered him in a good way.

"Of course, I remember you," Awissou said. "You came to the old compound often with your father, and I cannot forget your father and mine were first friends.

"I was a little older than you," Mautusan said, and I played chiefly with the older boys."

"You treated me well and with courtesy, not like some others," Awissou said.

"Who would have thought," Mautusan said, "you would become gbonuga of Allada."

"Is this a social call," Awissou noted, or is there something else on your mind?"

Mautusan explained to Awissou the task before him.

"You have taken a load upon you, Awissou said, "May Mawou protect you."

"I know you visit the court on occasion with the business of His Royal Majesty, Guezo," Mautusan said.

"Yes, the taxes I collect throughout the province," Awissou said, "and other matters of tribute.

"I have come to you," Mautusan said, "for some knowledge of how to comport myself at court."

"You must avoid anything showy and walk soft," Awissou said, "and be prepared for a long wait in the courtyard. There will be others of nobility and high status also waiting there to go before the court."

"I see," Mautusan said.

"It is beneath the king to address subordinates," Awissou said. And the migan [prime minister], concerns himself only with war. So you are most likely to be seen by the meu [second minister], who is in charge of all visitors at court. Once you are before the court, the slightest error in the protocol, the slightest hint of offense, and you may not leave there with your head intact."

"I wonder why I have taken on such a venture," Mautusan said. "I hope Legba's cunning finds me."

"Let not King Guezo need for the yovos to be seen at court because they are of low status," the gbonuga said, "I doubt the king would harm them, but he is known to keep whites of status with him a long time, to have someone to converse with and to learn their stories."

"But before you depart," the gbonuga said, "let us partake some of my European brandy to celebrate next we meet when you have prevailed against the things before you now."

"Thank you," Mautusan said, I'm in your debt," and he left there.

Mautusan's road led him through the farming country and toward the high plateau which Abomey sat. Then, finally, he walked through the city's gates and headed straight into the mouth of the Leopard.

Mautusan's suit was taken before the royal court after much formality, and he squatted on his haunches for several days in the courtyard waiting.

Finally, one morning, an officer came from the court to tell Mautusan he would have an audience with the meu at once. Whence he heard his name called, he advanced along the beaten ground and corridors of the palace. He stood before the meu a moment later, a big man with a menacing look about his face.

If Mautusan had not known such men during his travels, he would have felt fear. He prostrated himself before the meu, recalling the words of Lord Awissou, and clawed up dirt from the ground with both hands and poured it on his head as a sign of humility. He humbled his big voice to fit the circumstances. Then Mautusan explained the reason for being there.

"You are a wanderer," the meu said in an agitated voice, "who, on the one hand, dares return to Dahomey after many year's absence seeking the King's protection. And you have the further audacity also to seek protection for the whites who, in your own words, are of no importance even in their own country."

"I am calling upon the ancient precepts of the Dahomean kings," Mautusan said, as he repeated their words, 'I order you to allow even the poorest man to come before me, and the stranger who has no protectors in Da's Belly, so that I may help them.'

"The King also says." The meu retorted in a firm voice, 'I forbid my people to migrate from Da's Belly to another country, for a wanderer can never have a good love for the land.'

"I had to leave," Mautusan said, "for my life was in peril from the former king whose name we do not speak in Da's Belly."

Mautusan had hoped he would not have to refer to the former King, Adandozan. Maybe King Guezo was lurking in the shadows in earshot of his testimony. For one did not want to annoy a king with unpleasant memories of a time when he was called Prince Gakpe, and his mother and her household sent into slavery."

"Where are they now?" the meu said, "the whites and your two men."

"I left them at a place I played as a child," Mautusan said. (His words implied they were not in Dahomey, but there was some truth in his answer, for he played at Glidji as a child.)

"Why did you not bring them to Abomey?" the meu said.

"I did not want to presume on a matter I felt should be left to the prerogative of the court," Mautusan said.

"This one is too clever," the meu thought. "There's something about him, and under the show of humility, I see traces of a person of status. He could be trouble.

Mautusan began to have an uneasy feeling. Now he wondered what had possessed him to think he could outwit a high official of the royal court on his ground. The meu could not have survived as long as he had without a second sense when something wasn't right.

At that moment, the meu stopped questioning him. And, Mautusan lifted his head to see the meu walking toward an open corridor that seemed to lead into a big court. The meu began talking to another man about ten seasons younger than Mautusan, whose hue was a ways from black, wearing a loose robe of blue silk and a French hat. He carried himself in a manner that the meu should be honored to be in his presence.

"It must be King Guezo," Mautusan thought.

The meu returned and spoke words to Mautusan that surprised him. "You have been given leave to have your residence in Atogon, subject to Dahomean law. And let it be known, your whites are not to step beyond the province of Allada and that you and your people shall be like dogs that do not bark."

"Has King Guezo intervened on my behalf?" Mautusan thought. I guess Ku, death did not want me after all. I thank Mawou-Lissa, I thank Legba, the linguist of the Gods, and I thank Fa, who is Destiny, for the satisfactory outcome.

And that is how Mautusan and Robert and Patricia Wringle came to Dahomey.

As the day drew to an end, Adeoha felt it strange that all the livelong day, and well into the moonlight, her thoughts were about Mautusan, Robert, and Patricia, instead of the new road in her life, which perplexed her.

But little could Adeoha know. The priestesses and priests of the language drums said the magic kernels thrown by the diviner say the yovos and Mautusan's coming to Dahomey are connected to the oracle prophecy.

CHAPTER SIX

Two moons passed, the first rain fell in torrents across the land and nourished the earth once again. Planting the maize, cassava, beans, and peanuts is at hand, and later the millet, sorgo, and cotton seeds.

"The season that dances and life is reborn," Adeoha thought as she joined her family in the rite of sowing.

She basks in the feel of wet earth beneath her feet, as she reaches into the sack on one elbow, and with her right hand dropping the seeds into a hole made by her heel and covering them with a movement of the toe, the impact of it all a recognition of the earth gods, fertility, the sky gods, rain, and the ancestors, guidance.

Now, Adeoha took to her new business well, so she decided to continue instead of stopping. But the planting season was so inbred in the patterns of her life she devised a way to spend half her time planting and half with her business.

It's been two months since King Guezo launched another war. The people do not know where—Guezo conceals the place until within a day's march—but prayed to the gods and ancestors for the safety of the thousands called from their peaceful lives and the thousands of others who bring the supplies and other things and watch the soldier's back in hostile terrain.

Later that same day, Adeoha went to meet her three friends at the village square. She sent Gaye and Tsawi ahead with mats, and they prepared a small bamboo hut as a shield from the rain.

As Adeoha watched them leave, they reminded her of three instances on the road, the last one almost resulting in her demise and that of her troupe.

Just then, Sewextu arrived, and they greeted each other and embraced.

"Xontau daxo [first friend eldest], I'm glad you arrived before the others," Adeoha said. "I have words to share, only with my first friend. It concerns the troubles my band and I encountered on the road to and from Tori."

"Your words only exist between us, as it has always been, and will never know another's ears," Sewextu said.

"The first trouble was avoided by simply hiding in the brush and shrubs until the danger passed. But I came away from the near encounter feeling this is serious business, and I owed it to my people to leave them with their lives intact.

"I promoted the two best marksmen to shoot and moved Gaye and Tsawi to load and reload with the other two women. Whenever a free moment, I had them practice with the Danish single-shot muskets until red in the face, for it's a six-step process.

"Having four muskets blazing away, and then another four ready to fire, served us well when we fell into a fight with slavers, but a few well-placed volleys hit the flesh telling by the yells, sending our tormenters running off to find new game.

"The last time we left Tori, we were attacked by what seemed like a strong force. We were taking heavy fire during the ensuing skirmish, and the four of us with muskets in hand fell to our knees and began firing back; the other women of my troupe kept loading and reloading with great speed. But they kept coming.

"The attackers began to close in for the kill, and our firearms rendered useless. I pulled my assegai sword, and Isaige brandished her club and machete, ready for battle, and the other women followed suit. So there we were, a band of eight, readying for the onslaught, and all seemed lost.

"Then, all of a sudden, I heard the unmistakable, loud bark of Arabian muskets. As quickly as the battle had started, it had ended. The assailant's not killed fled, leaving some of their goods behind for our taking.

"I never knew who it was that saved us. But the Arabian muskets are as rare as gold in Dahomey. But I had a suspicion they were Tubutu's men sent secretly to watch over me because he possessed Arabian muskets with the same sound. He acquired them during his travels before he came to Dahomey. I have seen my father and his men practicing with these muskets many times while growing up.

"I understand," Sewextu said. "It is because of your father."

"Yes," Adeoha said. "If father mine wanted me to know, he would have spoken about it, and out of respect, I can't approach him on this matter.

As the sun made its departure from this side of the world, the rain stopped, but it was hot, and Adeoha and Sewextu took pleasure as they placed the mats over the wet earth and sat to await the others.

Although the three friends chosen by Adeoha were from upper-class families, they were not nobles, so theirs were positions of honor because Adeoha was a noble.

Soon they arrived. Adeoha embraced Agenu, xole-si-me [he who stands against the wall], daughter of Omowale, chief of a family guild of weavers. Unlike the first friend who is told everything, the second friend says, 'You should never tell another more than half of what you know.'

Then, Adeoha embraced Nneonee, her third friend, xonta gbo ka ta [the friend who stands on the threshold and is told nothing and must find out what she can on her own], daughter of Hwegajavi, head of the applique workers' guild.

"On our way here," Nneonee said, Agenu and I were talking about how well you are both doing since your time with the language drums society."

"There's a lot of talk among the women about your [Adeoha] business in Tori," Agenu said. "And Sewextu's songs are gaining in popularity throughout the provinces.

"Those things we call change in our lives, come from our fa," Sewextu said, "but fate is not fixed."

"Sewextu amazes us with the breadth of her storytelling," Adeoha said, the movements of her expression, her mastery of voice change, and now she comes with new songs and the verse, she will soon be the most sought after."

"How did things go for you in Abomey, Sewextu," Nneonee said, "My father's applique business is near the palace in Abomey. It's the center of our art forms, so you must have found it to your liking."

"It's a magnificent city," Sewextu said. "I met metal workers, wood-carvers, and ironworkers of status. I was especially beholden to the storytellers or ahajitos, and the 'song-give-birth-persons' and the verse makers; seeing them perform told me I have more to learn."

"You seem to have found every measure of what you looked for," Nneonee said.

"I was disappointed on one measure," Sewextu said. "I wasn't able to see the Mino. It is said they reach the highest realm as dancers, and they play all the musical instruments."

"The reason the Mino weren't there is that they are with King Guezo in another warring campaign," Adeoha said. "Much of Dahomey's revenue comes from selling the prisoners it takes into slavery across the sea."

"That is his fa," Sewextu said. That is what he does, like all his grandfathers or Aladahonu kings before him, Wegbaja, Akaba, Agaja, Tegbesu, and the others that followed. I don't admire that—how can I?

"But I do admire that he has ordered his chiefs and police in the provinces to ensure the peaceful and lawful coexistence of all Dahomeans—nobles, commoners, and slaves. And he has heightened and encouraged the arts.

"There are times we take our arts for granted. What would Dahomey be without song and dance, without drums and string instruments, without storytellers and verse makers, without applique and calabash carvers? Some rulers would deprive us of all of it. We can accuse King Guezo of many things, but this is not one of them."

"His Majesty holds many captives," Nneonee said, "but he is more interested in having enough men to till his fields than selling them to the white traders. And once they are selected, they are never sold and remain with the king the rest of their lives."

"In the past," Adeoha said, "the king's and their counselors pointed to the slave raids as a means to meet the heavy tax burden to the Ayo. But that reason no longer exists because Guezo freed us from the yoke of paying tribute to the Ayo. Yet, the slave raids continue and are more numerous than ever."

"When our army kills in far-off lands, we know it's wrong without emotion because our only witness is in words," Agenu said. "But our people witness in the flesh, the coffles making their trek from Abomey to the beach at Ouidah, and it saddens our hearts and the eyes of our people mist in whispers when they see the strength of Abeokuta in chains descending away."

"What is Abeokuta?" Nneonee said.

"A country many days journey from here." Agenu said, "Its people stand and fight our armies, giving not a quarter in return."

"It's been two moons since the King Guezo called for war and the soldiers and soldieresses embarked on the current campaign, Adeoha said. Where is our army now? What harm are they doing? Yes, many among us get some pleasure from all that we should detest.

"They say that our conquests make us great, and they say to the king and his councilors, attack this one and attack that one. But some people have begun to realize that they are the prey of the slave hunts and prolonged wars, and others go about endlessly as if these horrors do not exist or the fault lies with our victims.

"That is why today, Ku—death—sits upon me, a reminder of all the young men who have crossed the river as the result of needless wars to satisfy greed and the thirst for power."

"As true as the words spoken here today are, Sewextu said, the truth be told, we no longer have secret societies to outwit the corrupt. We do not have the power to quell the things we see as wrong.

"He who makes the gunpowder wins the battle. And the King has the gunpowder and the forges to make the weapons and the army to enforce his mandates, and we can only bear the burden of the atrocities committed in the name of our country.

"But there is a universal truth, the voice of Mawou, the self-existent one. Perhaps the men with the power to do so will always treat other men in this fashion, so it is upon us to pass the voice of Mawou down to our children and their children and hold the line that humanity will continue to follow a path in the light of the Creator."

"Enough talk of the esoteric things of life," Nneonee said. "Let us prepare for the Avogan [social dance] tonight. We go now to our houses, bathe, rub down with the aromatic plants, and put on our fine cloths and beads. Then we can meet the third hour from now at the court square and bedazzle the young lions."

"The young lions Nneonee speaks of is a single lion," Agenu said. "It is the tall, broad-shouldered Adewallye she speaks of." The friends joined together in laughter and danced in a ring around Nneonee, mimicking young lovers' games.

"We have held each other," Nneonee said, "and our lips have touched for a moment. That is all."

"That is all that she is telling us," Adeoha said, and the four of them heartily laughed as friends do. They parted ways and met later at the Avogan for a night of dancing and mischief.

*****

"Soon, another season of planting the seeds of life will give way to the grand harvest. I have made six treks to Allada,

Akpe, Tori, and back to Atogon. The profits from my business grow each time out, and the money I have loaned has been repaid. And when it hasn't, the borrowers have become pawns and labor in my new fields to repay their debt.

"And I can't forget my grandfather, Lord Ewansi. At first, he did not favor my new business, but when he learned from O'Gwumike how determined I was, he told me of a road that would take me through the farming country and the good wholesale markets near Allada.

"My grandfather, Lord Ewansi, put in my hand the clan totem [Awansou clan, owner of a mountain] to present to the gletanu's [the great cultivators]. Maybe these wholesale markets are not as big as the one in Djidja, above Abomey—but big enough for my needs as I bought many things there and resold them at the market in Tori at a good profit."

During the last moon, Adeoha's business took a decided upward turn and

set in motion a series of events that would
change her life forever.

Adeoha's last two times out on the road with her band, she crossed paths with experienced traders with stories of their travels. They breathed new energy into her with tales about the legendary markets beyond Dahomey where only the eminent traders and merchants in the precious stones dare show.

Now she was confident [femme malin], no one could get the best of her, and she would kill [idiom of Dahomey] at the chief trading towns of Dahomey: Ugbiya, Aladagbe, Nwacheme, Agbogbwe, and Hwedjisi. It was at these places; she would learn all that she needed. Then she would go beyond Dahomey.

Adeoha brought immense joy to the women of her band, telling them all roads to Tori would cease during June because of the heavy rainfall, and they would resume after the harvest. She singled out Gaye and Tsawi to tell them she would talk to her father about freeing them.

Adeoha also decided she would go before the women of Lamtaala's gybe after the harvest. There was much she could learn from these women. First, they were shrewd in business, told by their independent wealth and powerful lineages within Dahomean society.

Once the rains ended, the harvest began. So numerous were Lord Ewansi's fields that despite his workers and dokpwe, he had to reach out to the relatives of his wives as well as his married sons. But, even with that, he had to invite his distant kin who lived well to the north of Abomey. It brought Adeoha joy that many of those invited were kin she hadn't seen since they played together as children.

The harvest was of such magnitude that Lord Ewansi, with great ostentation and pride, caused the feasting to go on for two Dahomean weeks after the harvest ended, and he gave gifts to everyone for their help.

All through Ewansi's compound and extended compounds, there was much eating, drinking, laughter, and dancing. The music of gongs, cymbals, flageolets filled the air, and every type of percussion instrument made in Dahomey thundered the intricate rhythms of Afrikan music through the night.

The yam harvest is a meaningful time for all Dahomeans. Adeoha and the women of each compound enjoyed the festive yam ceremonies honoring the Goddesses Yalode and Tokpodun. The women danced and sang, and the children feasted on yams, ram meat, and chicken, and later they went dancing through the village.

Adeoha was sure that never in her life had she experienced greater joy or felt more in harmony with the forces of nature.

*****

The day after Adeoha and her troupe returned to Atogon from their first time out on the road again since the harvest ended, she prepared to go before Lamtaala's gybe.

Adeoha sat on a low stool in the corner, anticipating the comments of Lady Alunje about her readiness to trade in gold and silver and other costly things.

"In all practical matters as a trader, Lady Alunje said, you may not have one person your equal. You have proved that with your successes at the wholesale markets and the big market at Tori. But that is not enough. Your knowledge of the storyteller's art is insufficient for trading gold, silver, brass, and other things.

"There's a knack to it and many subtleties to be learned. A trader with cunning will outsmart a trader with little experience every time, with a fantastic story of the origin of the object or some other ruse. But, on the other hand, a trader wishing to make a mark in the famous markets must be a famous liar."

The next afternoon, Adeoha received a visit from her first friend Sewextu. Adeoha told her what had happened at the gybe.

"What Lady Alunje is saying, Sewextu said, "is not unlike what we heard at the storytelling sessions as children. It carries the meaning you need to have as many stories as there are fa tales."

"Well, that's a lot of stories," Adeoha said and laughed. "The elders say the world will not end until all the fa stories have been told."

"Lady Alunje is also saying the business you seek is not like the one you are involved in now. Now, the goods you sell have no stories to tell. But the business you seek, the stories you tell about the articles you hold will enhance their value. It is the same for the things you think about buying. So you have to be clever about what you hear."

"You see much of life through the storyteller's art," Adeoha said.

"And hopefully through the eyes of our ancestors," Sewextu said.

"Tell me a story Sewextu," Adeoha said, "that I can learn from."

"The one that comes to mind is an old moralizing tale," Sewextu said: 'Why there are liars, adulterers, and thieves.'

"The long story is about the liar and only makes a vague reference to the other two," Sewextu said. "This is another Dada Segbo story, the mythic king who reigned in the early days of the world:"

*****

The bird called *gangan* went to a place called Fetome, the city of Ife, in Nigeria. The bird said to Dada Segbo that there at Fetome, they knew how to speak. So Dada Segbo called Vulture.**

Dada Segbo said, "You are always at Fetome. Have you found there a thing called speech?" And he said, "When you go there again, then tell the others to send me speech without delay.

**Dahomean Narrative: A Cross-Cultural Analysis ~ By Melville J. Herskovits & Francis S. Herskovits Explanatory and Moralizing Tales ~ Pgs. 410-412

So Vulture went to tell the king of Fetome what the king, Dada Segbo, had said. Vulture said, "He asks you to send him speech." The king of Fetome said, if Dada Segbo wished to look after his children, they would come and teach Dada Segbo speech. So vulture returned and said to the king, "The king of Fetome agreed to send you some of his children, and they will teach you to speak."

Dada Segbo said, "Good."

When Vulture left Fetome, they gave him three rolled-up mats. He took them up with his claws, and he brought the three to Dada Segbo. When the king unrolled the mats, he saw three small boys.

These boys grew up. Now the eldest went after other men's wives. But, there must not be a man who goes after other men's wives in the king's house. The second began to rob. But in the king's house, there cannot be thieves. The third was on good terms with the king's senior wife.

Now, the king had a long beard. So the third said to the king's senior wife, "You must get some hair from the king's beard, and I will make you a charm that will cause you to be loved."

Next, he went to the king. He said, "Tonight, your senior wife will try to kill you. So when they went to sleep, the king did not fall asleep. The senior wife came with a knife to cut off some hair from the king's beard. The king caught her by the wrist, and he began to call. They bound the woman.

Now, as the woman had a grown son working in the field, the young man from Fetome went to tell him that the king had bound his mother and would kill her. He said, "if you are prepared to save her, you must bring your gun and your knife; for your father is ready for war."

Then, he went to the king, and he said, "As you bound this woman, her son has gone with the news to all his brothers, and they are coming with guns to kill you."

When the king heard this, he called together all his people, and he told them that his son was about to make war on him.

Now, all these people were before the King's doorway awaiting the arrival of the son.

When the young man and his friends approached the king's house and saw so many people gathered there, he began to shoot, for he thought his father was ready for war. So they began to fight.

The liar climbed up a tree, and he called out, "Silence! Those who come from the fields, stop firing! Those who are here at the house, stop firing!" "He asked, Where is the king?"

But the king had already run away to hide. So, they went to find the king.

The liar said, "The king asked for three children to care for. But it is a child, and only one, who conquered his kingdom. He said, "The king had asked for three liars, but I alone showed myself able to break his kingdom. One can never watch over the people of Fetome.

So the king had Vulture come, and he said, "Now since you were the one who brought these people from Fetome, you must be the one to return them." So Vulture took them back to Fetome.

*****

"So it was the liar who had caused the war," Sewextu said.

"Yes, I recall the story," Adeoha said.

"Now, you must look deep in the story, Sewextu said. And learn from what it tells you to make yourself a better trader. The liar had a plan, as you must have a plan. First, he used the fact that the king had a long beard and a king is always looking around him for one who might want to kill him. Next, he went to see the king's senior wife and learned she wanted to be loved.

"So the young man came up with a story that could make this happen. Just as you must come up with a story for your prospective buyer or seller where they must have it or leave it at all costs."

"I am capable of doing this," Adeoha said.

"There is more," Sewextu said. Just as the liar told another story to the woman's son and then another to the king, you can enhance your tale a third time, then a fourth time. For example, suppose it is a gold chain, you can say it had many owners, and the strange circumstances it came into your possession."

Now, Adeoha gathered her people, prepared her goods, and made ready for the market at Atogon that morning.

"Come, Adeoha said to her people, for today is a good day to begin our venture. So let us go and find our road."

Four Dahomean weeks went by, and Adeoha returned from Tori that morning and spent the day trading in the marketplace at Atogon. When she got to Tubutu's compound and home, she found Sewextu waiting. As the night approached, they sat amid the grove of baobab trees in the compound.

"The first time I went on the road after we spoke," Adeoha said, "I focused on the things you told me. At first, I listened, and then I began asking the traders and merchants I crossed paths with about the stories and terrains of their countries.

"You are wise to study the words of those you came in contact with," Sewextu said.

"My second time out from which I have just returned," Adeoha said, "I began to tell my stories, and I was surprised how well they were received. One particular buyer couldn't stop laughing as he said, 'your price is extravagant, but well worth it, after hearing the story surrounding it.'

"A passing merchant on his way to Abomey told a story, which became the latest gossip, of a girl-child from Allada who bested several older, experienced traders," Sewextu said. "The story was made to sound better with the person coming from Allada than our small village. But I was sure it was you.

"Yes, there were three times I was able to hold my own in the buying and selling of brass and silver objects, Adeoha said. But the story I will treasure because it was my first, I was able to sell a Persian scimitar with a hilt of gold at a great advantage in price despite paying a lot for it.

"I told a group of traders, the scimitar passed from many owners and found its way to Egypt, and then across the desert to Timbuctoo, and from there to Oyo country."

"You have some imagination," Sewextu said, "you have learned well. I will not spoil your story by asking more. I like your version of it better."

"During recent times, as you know," Adeoha said, "I have met with the women of my mother's gybe as often as they could put up with me. But the last time we met, Lady Alunje said to me, 'When you have told enough good stories, your words will come back to you from the mouths of others.'

181

"I think Lady Alunje is telling you," Sewextu said, "you have satisfied what is necessary to trade in the great markets."

"At night," Adeoha said, "I'm going to begin going to the storytelling sessions at the compounds.

"You seem to have captured the essence of the tale," Sewextu said. "Is this a way to add more bush to the fire?

"I don't know," Adeoha said. "I'm just following my head.

"It seems you are entering the realm of the dance and the world of story-telling," Sewextu said in astonishment and laughed. "Next, you will be making verse."

"No, Adeoha said, these crafts are not mine, "but I would like to give a dance before the gybe," Adeoha said, "to thank the women for helping me."

"I'm going to Abomey with my group for a week," Sewextu said. So I will see you when I return."

The very next day, as Adeoha walked outside Tubutu's compound, she began to hear a faint drumbeat in her head, and she envisioned a Legba tale, then she stopped walking and danced to it, and thought nothing of it.

Adeoha's following day was brimming, with the last of the harvest and the planting of the seeds for the second harvest in two moons.

That night, Adeoha appeared at her first storytelling session and asked to present a dance. The narrator for the session agreed, knowing that Adeoha was a personage of nobility.

As Adeoha danced, she could hear the drumbeat once more, but no fa story came to her head, as it had on the way to the stream. But, it turned out well; she was a big hit with the children and her age mates because of her dance's complicated rhythms and patterns.

The next day, Adeoha was told about a storytelling session at another compound in the village that night and went there. When

Adeoha arrived, the children were involved in a riddling game, for the elders saw it as an exercise in memory training. The elders told Adeoha she could present her dance after the riddling session.

When Adeoha began to dance, she could hear the faint drumbeat for the third time, but a fa story played in her head, and she danced to it.

A young man present began to beat the drum to the same rhythm as in Adeoha's head. The children thought it was a part of the riddling session. They hollered, 'Loa wi and the rites of sowing'—the same fa story that was in Adeoha's head and her dance— thinking they had solved the riddle, several of the children happily shouted, 'the story is about a young girl and her life on the land.'

Sewextu, afresh from her time at Abomey, returned to Atogon at midafternoon and went to Tubutu's compound to see Adeoha.

"She has gone to the river," Lamtaala said. "She said you would know where."

"I know the place," Sewextu said, "I thank you, Lady Lamtaala," bowing respectfully and left there.

"How have you come with the gybe dance and the storytellers," Sewextu said.

"My dance for the gybe is granted," Adeoha said.

"What about the storytelling sessions," Sewextu said.

Adeoha explained what had happened on her way to the stream and her times at the storytelling sessions.

"I was presenting a dance," Adeoha said. There was nothing else to say, and I have many dances for the storytelling sessions.

"I wonder what the elders thought seeing the children riddling and throwing their answers at you," Sewextu said. "

"The children and those a little older couldn't have known it any better if I shouted it out to Hevioso," Adeoha said.

"The first time you were alone and walking, and you heard the drumbeats and saw a fa tale in your head. The next time you listened to the drumbeats, but nothing came to your head, Sewextu gibed her, and they laughed as they often did. "And when you performed at Lady Lamtaala's gybe, you once again heard the drumbeats, and a story not only came to your head, but the audience recited it back to you.

Adeoha at any other time would appreciate her first friend's gibes, but not now. "I have to choose the dance I will give at the gybe, and I have gone through all the movements and rhythms we learned during our initiation days. I have to choose one —
"

"You will find it," Sewextu said, or it will find you with the drum beats.

"I hope so, Adeoha said.

"It is a good story you told or danced at the storytelling session," Sewextu said. "A young girl goes from sowing to the market, then buys her own cloths, and becomes a market woman, and is always on the lookout to increases to her wealth the rest of her life."

"Maybe I can get more from the dance story," Adeoha said. "We all know the Legba myths, the master of the crossroads, the thing that cannot happen, coincidence, cause and effect, accident, and besides all his other mischief.

"It will make good verse," Sewextu said, "seeing what dance you choose, or better still, which dance chooses you."

"I'll be at the language drums compound," Sewextu said, "there's a lot I can still learn there."

CHAPTER SEVEN

The day of Adeoha's dance at the Society
had come. The evening fell across the
Afrikan sky as Adeoha walked through the
compound. Lady Alunje greeted her and
Tawasha, the drummer boy. Adeoha had met
him at the storytelling sessions. She liked
how he beat the drum for her dance, and he
was younger than she was.

Tawasha, no more than twelve, stood in
awe of the spacious compound, for he was
the son of a tenant farmer. He reminded her
of a childhood friend who was also the son
of a tenant farmer who crossed the river
during one of the King's slave raids.

The women of the society began to arrive
in their ornamented hammocks, stepping
down with the help of their bearers to the
clatter of their jewelry against the laughter
of a pack of hyenas out on the savanna.

The members of the society were having
their last meeting before their big dance, so

there must have been more than one hundred people present.

Dahomey is a land that abounds with mutual aid societies. All Dahomeans belong to at least one unless they could not afford the lavish ceremonies that only the rich could afford, expensive weddings, showy gifts, without which they could not walk with their heads held high. Therefore, each member contributes a fixed sum of money regularly for their time in need.

The Society of Lady Alunje and Lady Lamtaala was different. These women were all independently wealthy, and they found pleasure in giving extravagant celebrations attended by the notables and personages of high rank. A bokonon was called in, for no undertaking of importance could begin without first divining. The bokonoe cast the sacred kernels, and they fell favorably and told the dance would be successful.

The women completed their meeting by first invoking a song to the ancestors and asking the old ones to watch over their paths, continue to guide them toward the good things in life, and help them increase their wealth so they could leave their children more than they had inherited.

The rustle of the trees caused some among the crowd to whisper that the rainbow serpent Aido Hwedo had come down from the heavens in the mists to rest amid the surrounding trees. Native oil lamps lit up the night, and the members and guests sat and awaited the surprise entertainment.

Lady Alunje addressed her fellow members, speaking of Adeoha's time with the Language of the Drums and the good times she had spent among the gybe learning the nuances of the trader's occupation. She wishes to give us a dance from what she has learned, so here with us now, Lady Adeoha, daughter of Tubutu and Lamtaala.

As Adeoha listened, her simple heart was singing softly with excitement, and she pulled her three souls to her. She stepped forward and climbed atop the attoh, built for the occasion by Lady Alunje.

Adeoha stepped forward and climbed atop the attoh. Then, she set out on a dance—with a sequence and movements rarely seen beyond the compound of the language drums.

"What is this? Adeoha thought. I cannot dance the way it is in my head. It's impossible. But slowly, she began stepping, unsure of herself but keeping the rhythm, now she began to dance, and she could see the heho [be it fable or parable].

The audience looked at Adeoha as if she was at a loss. But the story continued to fill her, and she could feel how to dance to it. As impossible as it seemed, she began moving, moving fast, and her bent knees kept her closer to the ground, and her foot speed revealed a new rhythm, and her movements pushed the boy to beat the drum within the dance, and the onlookers took notice.

Now Adeoha began to enchant her hosts, her long, flowing purple dress dazzling in the red moonlit sky. She beat out new rhythms, and she leaped or soared high, and then settled back to earth, gently touching the earthen ground, and her dance was a language, and it spoke of a young girl, selling foodstuffs in the marketplace.

Then she aroused the spectators by her arm and leg movements and footfalls—they were not always even, yet her dance steps were. She had cut the beat and found it, which left the audience in anticipation.

Adeoha's expression changed, and the spectators knew that a young girl saw something that pleased her very much. By the way, the girl craned her neck—considering her height—she was looking at someone very tall, perhaps a boy her age. The girl approached the boy with dancing steps understood to be an invitation to come with her.

Adeoha's dance revealed the boy had rejected her advances. She whirled around him, removing her garments, and stood naked, and the boy turned her away. Then she fell to the earth, pulling the boy down with her, he tried to rise again, but the girl lay with him. When the sex act was over, he died.

Adeoha's movements caused the illusion she was at the burial ground where the boy lay. And the spectators began to understand they might be seeing a new appeal. Then there were some in the audience who recognized the story, and it spread among them.

"It's the cult house," a voice yelled out.

"She's the girl who tempted the cult initiate to violate the law of Vodu," another woman hollered.

Adeoha, at this point, knew that some within the audience were interpreting her dance as she envisioned it.

The girl's gesture and expression showed her bowing to a priest who had entered and ordered the girl bound. Instead, the girl slid to the earth, performing a dance spin with unordinary balance at earth level, defying the priest.

And the onlookers yelled, while others sang, and their voices seem to bring down the sky, and their well-remembered and favorite words of the story echoed through the compound: "Do not bother to bind me. I am here." The girl remained seated beside her dead lover.

Now the girl rolled onto her shoulders and brought forth her feet above her. She kicked out and rose to a standing position and began a series of supple movements that involved her entire body, the undulation of the hips, and all the isolations she had learned from the language drums.

And now Adeoha's energy accentuates the drum rhythm of the young drummer, and the drum segment signals the entrance of the rest of the characters in the dance story. Her flowing footwork made the act of walking a dance. She drew the audience's participation, a tradition in Dahomean storytelling, emphasizing the interplay between narrator and audience, but in Adeoha's case, dancer and audience.

As the story goes, the words of the vodun: "if you wish the boy to come back to life, then bring three bundles of firewood, palm oil, dig a hole before the temple of the

Vodu and place these things in the hole."
There they were to put the boy's body.

Adeoha's gesture and expression took on
the appearance of asking, "Who among you
dare to enter the fire? Your courage will
save his life, and you both shall live."

A woman in the crowd proudly called
out, "The boy's name is Hundjo."

Adeoha swooped to the ground, rose, and
walked toward the fire as she assumed the
proud walk of Hundjo's mother.

As Hundjo's mother neared the flames,
she said, "No, I cannot. If I do not die, I will
live to bear another son.

Next, Hundjo's brother went toward the
fire, but he, too, lost heart.

Then, Hundjo's first friend turned away
from the flames.

Now, Adeoha danced the part of the girl,
Ahwala, who had caused Hundjo's death.
She took out from her sack all the articles
used in burial rites, a small calabash, two

sticks for cleaning the teeth, two pipes, tobacco, and matches.

But it was at this point the audience came together, maybe brought on by their recognition of the burial scene, they knew the girl's words that followed, and their voices called out the next passage, "If I do not go into the fire, I will not be able to live with my soul," Ahwala said. "I must find the courage to save my friend

Ahwala danced about the fire; by the way she recoiled, the audience knew the pyre had reached blazing proportions. Then, she circled the flames with unhurried care, made the supreme sacrifice, and entered the fire. In a few minutes, the two came out alive. All the villagers began to beat the drums and dance in the story, and great jubilation ensued.

Adeoha's dance played the words: "From this day on, the initiation ceremony must be concluded in three years instead of eight. Because of their disobedience, the initiation period was shortened. The young girl's courage and defiance moved both the Vodu and Death to pity. They took the young girl and gave her to Hundjo to marry." And with that, Adeoha's dance ended.

"As the people were leaving, a voice in the crowd said, "I don't know how Lady Alunje did it, but the dance was excellent, and the way some of us echoed out the story as if vying to see who could tell it best, that was grand."

"Maybe, when the first person told what heho or story it was," a second voice said, "everybody joined in. We have heard the story often; it brings back memories."

"We enjoyed the sunshine and rain," another voice echoed, "and we laughed together, something we don't do a lot of these days.

"You all saw what I saw," the first woman said, "the dance connected with the story throughout, especially the burial rite, and the spirit of the moment must have touched the boy for him to beat the drum-like he did."

Adeoha found Tawashu, and they headed for the hammock Tubutu had sent for her, and she took the boy home. Once she was home, her mind was heavy with thought, and she knew sleep was impossible. She had hardly begun to knock at Lamtaala's door when her mother invited her to come in.

"I've been waiting for you," Lamtaala said.

"Tell me, Mother," Adeoha said| "What have you to say about my dance?"

"Truth to tell, I was surprised," Lamtaala said. "I was not aware it was to be that story."

"It was a surprise to me as well," Adeoha said.

"There have been many changes in your life since your time with the Language of the Drums," Lamtaala said. "And no sooner have you started one profession than you look to begin another. Now, this new dance of yours seems to have a life of its own."

"The things you speak of are unusual," Adeoha said, "but they are not so much out of the ordinary."

"How did you come by your story?" Lamtaala asked.

"I planned to perform a simple dance about sowing, that is all," Adeoha said. Then I could hear a drumbeat within me, and I danced to it."

"Listen, Daughter mine," Lamtaala said, "I am not one to see miracles behind every tree. Your story was one of young love, which is not unusual from one as young as you. Have you not wished one day to find your true love and wed. That alone is enough for the story to have come from your head and not the Vodu or the ancestors as some people are saying."

"As you say, Mother," Adeoha said. "Perhaps the story was in my head all along. And yes, I look to wed one day, but not yet. First, I would like to add weight to my name as you have."

"Let us change the subject for now," Lamtaala said, "for only time will tell us these things."

"As I have told you before," Lamtaala said, "it seems that even in this instance, you could not help but express a story that could be seen as troublesome to the authority of the King.

"That was not my intention," Adeoha said.

"Your story was one of defiance," Lamtaala said. "It rewards disobedience."

"I wish I could give a dance for the people of Da's Belly," Adeoha said, filled with these sayings."

Lamtaala looked at her. "Foolish child of mine, it was once a small thing, the innocent chatter of a child, but you are no longer a child, and Da's Belly can be unforgiving.

Adeoha leaned over and kissed her mother's cheek. "Why do mothers so often imagine a bush is burning when it is not."

"It is our Fa, I guess," Lamtaala said.

Adeoha left her mother on that note and went to her room, where she found a night of peaceful sleep.

The next day, Adeoha went to meet Sewextu at their favorite spot near the river. Sewextu listened to her firsts friend's telling of her dance story at Lamtaala's gybe.

"I wish to have been there to see your dance, Sewextu said. But I was there with you at the language drums, so I know how it is with you.

"The senior members of the language drums have been aware of your dance at the storytelling sessions, and they are mystified. "I have overheard the chief priestess say the ancestors of the oracle are still with you, and their presence and your dance are getting stronger."

"Soon, they will hear about my performance for Lady Alunje and the gybe," Adeoha said.

"I would not be surprised if they already know," Sewextu said.

"What else is on your mind?" Adeoha said.

"It is the same for me as always this time of year," Sewextu said, "The contest against Allada. Just once, I would like to bring them down from atop the high stool they sit."

"The Allada troupe treat all their rivals with equal disdain," Adeoha said, so don't take it personally. It probably comes from the way they smash every village they meet.

"They have an arrogant way about them," Sewextu said, "They are far more insolent than their performance is good."

"While their words and songs bite deep into the shortcomings of their rivals," Adeoha said, "it does bring forth much laughter."

"I also laugh at their gibes," Sewextu said, "even louder than you, Adeoha."

"A lot of it could be old-fashioned Dahomean pride," Adeoha said. "this rebuke by your fellow artists stings a little, especially since their songs often become hits among our age mates."

"Yes," Sewextu agreed. "I don't seem to be able to compose songs that mock and ridicule others."

"That is because compassion rules your heart," Adeoha said. "And that is why your dance, story-telling, and making verse are gaining you stature throughout the provinces. Our age-mates are calling you ajisumo; your heart understands much."

"All I know," Sewextu said, "when the contest has ended, and we are alone together, they look at us as if we were dirt. So I want to turn the tide on them just once and see their faces on the walk back to Allada when they are not the center of everyone's attention."

By sunset the next day, both Adeoha and Sewextu departed Atogon. Adeoha and her people set out for Allada, Akpe, and Tori. And Sewextu went to Ajajou to work with the clay at her family's pottery business.

During the next Dahomean week, Sewextu returned to Atogon, a light rain sprinkled the earth, and she enjoyed the good, cool weather. She was not content to accept defeat and humiliation again at the hands of the Allada troupe. But what could she do but pray to the ancestors and Vodun to turn her down a road where she would find an awaiting answer.

Somewhere in the distance, she could hear the sweet sound of a flute, and it was coming closer. She watched as some fifty men accompanied by twenty or so women passed nearby. She did not know them, so they must have come from far to break ground or build a house or thatch a roof for someone in Atogon.

The fine, big guy with the staff must be their chief or dokpewega. He walks proudly, his head held high, for he not only commands but also has charge of the burial rites of his village, not unlike the dokpwega of Atogon.

Sewextu found joy in the many dokpwe and all the mutual aid societies of Da's Belly. There was a light in her eyes and a smile on her face as she thought of the sick old man who could not tend his fields; his son and his dokpwe did it for him freely.

"This has been our way, always," Sewextu thought.

Sewextu began to walk behind the visitors, drawn by curiosity and the stirring music that took her mind from Allada. Once the dokpwe reached its destination, Sewextu followed them into the compound.

Sewextu had walked upon a good contest between two dokpwes and in the most arduous labor of all: the roofing of a house. However, the men look at their efforts as not burdensome but as recreation.

The compound head was a man of modest means, so the work for him would not be entirely free of cost, but his payment would be small compared to the labor involved.

Sewextu smiled and looked about the compound where the older men of the village were preparing thatch while the young men were busy bringing supplies or working with the bamboo poles or stripping the palm ribs. The village maidens whispered excitedly as they looked at the men, most of whom were well-muscled and as slender as a loko sapling.

The competition began with loud cheers. Each dokpwe had upwards of fifty men. They performed their labor with the expenditure of much muscular energy, accompanied by the rhythms of their dokpwe songs and the shouts of encouragement by the village maidens'

The first task was to erect the ridge pole and the frame which held the roof, and the second was to raise the interlacing frames of bamboo poles.

The contest began to heat up as the cross pieces of palm rib were laid on the poles reaching down from the ridge of the wall. There was much rivalry to see which team would be the first to get to the ridge pole.

The rest of the dokpwe watched and cheered, accompanied by drums, gongs, and rattles. No one worked for too long before being relieved to join in the singing until his turn came again.

The visiting group took the lead, and their laughter and songs of derision at the expense of the locals grew loud, but as the home team began to narrow the gap, the cheering of the crowd was deafening.

The good-natured taunting aroused in Sewextu thoughts about the upcoming contest with Allada. The taunting she and her troupe would face would be unsparing and relentless, and she could not think of a way to avoid it.

The best of the contest would not begin until after noonday. But she had to leave because of business elsewhere. As she got further away from the sounds of the competition, her mind became empty, and from that emptiness sprang an idea.

CHAPTER EIGHT

A few days later, Sewextu called together the six members of her dance gybe. Her prestige was such that among the members, she was elected president. This particular gybe was for promising females in the arts. When they had assembled at the stream called Azili, she addressed her sisters who would perform with her against their rivals from Allada.

"Sisters mine," Sewextu said, "I call upon you to push me toward something close to my heart, as I know it is close to yours. I can live with losing to Allada, but not as we did last year. Their status is the same as ours, but they treat us like we are nothing."

The members of the group were not surprised by Sewextu's words. They knew it had bothered her since their last meeting and that this year would be the same.

"My friend Adeoha," Sewextu said, "has made a dance. It is a different kind of dance, and if you can trust me, and you are willing to let Adeoha come into our troupe and take the lead, I think we have a chance to do something that Dahomeans will long remember."

The members were confused by her words, for she asked them to bring in a new member with a new vision, which would mean throwing aside all the hard work for something new. And even if they agreed, so little time remained before the match with Allada.

But their thoughts were tempered by Sewextu's high status and their trust that she would not ask them to do something that she did not think possible. Of all those present other than Sewextu, only Dzifa, daughter of the beekeeper Nogaye, had seen Adeoha's dance story.

"I think what Sewextu says could put us in a popular way among our people," Dzifa said. "I have seen the dance she speaks off."

"Can she throw insults upon the real or imagined shortcomings of our rivals," Nnedi said, "or can she bring new words and verse that will bring laughter from the crowd and sway the judges in our favor."

"No, she cannot do any of these things, Sewextu said. But I believe when Adeoha dances and the drums respond, some of the crowd will begin to interpret the story she weaves, and from there, others will know. So, hopefully, it will gain the participation of a large number of the audience.

"And what do you base this on," Nnedi said.

"Although I did not see it with my eyes," Sewextu said, "the last two times, once at the storyteller's session and again at Lamtaala's gybe, in both instances, the audience responded by telling the story of her dance."

"We are told," Afua said, "it will be a big turnout as in past years according to our tradition. They will remember us by it." And all the members agreed they would welcome Adeoha to their society.

"We will not address the audience," Sewextu said. "Instead, the dance will speak for us and tell our story. We'll place ourselves across the attoh and well behind and away from Adeoha and accompany her rhythms with our own that we have practiced.

"The seven of us fluttering about in the beat, as long as we hold the line, should be seen as a good compliment to Adeoha's dance," Dzifa said.

The next day, Adeoha sat beneath a baobab tree beside her first friend, Sewextu, with not a care in the world.

"I had a joyous time with my cunning grandmother, Lady Glyya, yesterday," Adeoha said. She spent the whole afternoon explaining how she moved the palm trees from Lord Ewansi's sib to a family property; thereupon, Lady Lamtaala could inherit them, and I will inherit from her.

"Our laws of inheritance," Sewextu said, are a complicated business."

"You have that look of something else on your mind, again," Adeoha said.

"Recently, I watched a competition between a dokpwe from Atogon and another country," Sewextu said. "It awoke in me the feeling that I must bring you into my dance troupe for the contest against Allada."

"Surely, this is one of your well-meaning gibes," Adeoha said.

"As your first friend," Sewextu said, it is my duty. "

"I don't want to hear about duty," Adeoha said, and the friends hugged, and you could hear a light laugh between them, for their friendship had been tested many times.

"When we recently met, you did not speak on it. But you walked like your dance story at Lady Lamtaala's gybe left you in a good way," Sewextu said.

"I cannot join you," Adeoha said. "I am not a dancer, it is not my occupation, and it is not my art."

"Your heho of Loa wi and the rites of sowing," and the dance story about the women who tempted the initiate, say differently," Sewextu said.

"But that came from the children at the night stories and the women of my mother's gybe," Adeoha said. But the two thousand people expected there would be mostly our-age mates, and we will not hear the last of it if we should fall.

"I have seen you dance at the language drums throughout our initiation period," Sewextu said, "if that is the worst of it, then we are in a strong place."

"It seems like another mischief or another adventure to me," Adeoha said, and these stories are minor, which leave us hot in gaming."

"A game of adji or ako anyone," Sewextu said, all gibing aside, we don't know what story if any will find the moment."

"There's no category for my dance," Adeoha said.

"Then we shall make one," Sewextu said.

"Those of the language drums, find time to talk about the honor you have brought to our house," Sewextu said.

"The only thing I have done," Adeoha said, "is to continue with the movements and exercises because I like doing them."

"It was just a few moons ago," Adeoha said, "when you told me of your intention to seek membership in the society, and you involved me in it. And this time, you want to reign over Allada in the contest with me at your side.

"Yes," sister mine," Sewextu said. "I think you will come to see the affair with Allada as a challenge," Sewextu said.

"I think you have come, my first friend," Adeoha said, "just to annoy me with mischief.

"We have had some good times together," Sewextu said, "all the wild schemes of yours that I have accompanied you on."

"I can't explain my dance story. It's weird," Adeoha said. "For that reason, I will join you and the sisters of the dance for the contest against Allada."

*****

A few days passed, Adeoha went to the forest for firewood. Before leaving, she thought, "I should make the little sacrifices and rituals to the Vodu, for I have spent enough time learning them, and who can say what is possible and what is not."

When she reached the forest, she began to wield the ax with her accustomed swiftness and sang to the rhythm of her movements. Her mind began to think about all the new things in her life: her business at Tori and her new mercantile venture, her new fields and the good harvest, and the money she loaned was repaid, and even those who couldn't repay her brought a profit, by pawning themselves for labor in her fields until the debt was paid.

Then, just as the contest with Allada came to her head, the ax came down and through its target and struck the earth and bounced near her leg. She was amazed at how close it came until she saw the blood running down her leg. After that, she made medicine from an infusion of leaves and earth in the forest and covered the wound with a salve. Now she occupied her thoughts solely with the task at hand.

Later that day, when Adeoha entered Tubutu's compound, she could see Patricia viovo, sitting under a palm tree. The two friends embraced and walked together as Adeoha put away her burden. Then they walked to their secret place in the small forest beyond the anya grove. There they had come often to introduce each other to their cultures.

"It's always so peaceful here," Patricia said. "I'll miss it."

"What are you saying," Adeoha said.

"Robert and I have been thinking about our families and friends more often and wondering what's going on in America since we left. We have decided it's time to go home," Patricia said.

"You have been with me and watched me grow tall, Adeoha said, "We met when I was a child soon to turn twelve, and now I am a woman soon to have sixteen seasons on the earth. We have shared the treasure of good times and knowledge.

"We hope to leave about this time next year, after the second harvest," Patricia said. "By that time, Robert and I hope to have adopted Atedeku and Okpewa as our son and daughter. They have contributed to our constant joy and brought meaning to our lives as members of our household. But to make it legal, we have to find Atedeku, a wife, and Okpewa, a husband. Then they can inherit our property when we leave."

"Yes, that will set a precedent," Adeoha said. But the complexities of the inheritance law won't fully begin until Atedeku and Okpewa have sons and daughters, and they marry, and their children inherit.

"We have started," Patricia said. "The elders in the law are helping us. It's complicated and tiresome to learn, but worth it. They are both young, and we know they will increase the wealth we have left them for their children."

"It's better than have it go to the King's estate or that of the Gbonuga of Allada," Adeoha said.

"I remember the incredible feeling both Robert and I had to remain in Afrika," Patricia said.

"You have not been away a long time," Adeoha said, "You will feel at home again in less than a moon.

"You're right, Adeoha," Sewextu said, "five years is not much time.

"Your leaving Dahomey," Adeoha said, "only adds to the recent changes in my life."

"What will you do when you are home?" Adeoha said. "Will you continue to teach the things you have taught me?"

"Because of how easy you took to it," Patricia said, "maybe I'll open a school. I don't think teaching is it for me. My fight is for higher education for women. Although it takes time for issues to waver through

America, I feel good things are happening, and It will be a good time to return."

"We have many things remaining between us before you leave," Adeoha said. "We have learned a lot from each other, and I will miss that."

The beginning of the short dry season was thought of by Dahomeans as the beginning of a new season in their lives, which added to the pomp of the Grand Festival. The featured entertainment on the first day will commence in the evening and continue until the first hour past midnight. The contest between Allada and Atogon will begin on the evening of the second day and followed by the big dance starting precisely at midnight.

The opening ceremonies began with a parade through the village, with crowds of singing, dancing, and drumming men and women. They were dressed in cloths of dazzling colors, as were the acrobats, jugglers, and fire-eaters that followed them.

Next came the men on their horses—unusual because good horses were hard to find in Dahomey because of the tsetse fly—performing a repertoire of tricks, and men and women threw their torches high in the sky deftly catching them before they touch the earth.

Finally, the dokpwes and mutual aid societies paraded and danced under their applique banners. Their cadences mingled with the sounds of Mother Afrika and echoed like a warm summer breeze across the land.

The evening of the second day is at hand. The Allada troupe started the festivities with their well-honed vignette of satire, which was a prelude to what was to come, all of which cause the spectators to roar with approval. The depth of their wit was biting and held their rivals up for ridicule and laughter at every turn, and nothing was off-limits from them, which continued for a good hour and a half.

As Adeoha watched, she could not imagine how she and her sisters of the dance could compete with them, and she wondered how she had let Sewextu talk her into it.

Now, here she is, moments away from walking out on the attoh before the giant crowd, in number.

"Everything has happened so fast," Adeoha thought, "perhaps this will be the end of it."

During the days leading up to the festival, Adeoha exercised in the manner of the Language of the Drums and practiced all the dance maneuvers she had learned there. Thereupon, she tried to work themes into her dance stories that would mock Allada. She listened for the drumbeats, but they were not to be heard.

But her thoughts kept going back to when she was chopping wood in the forest and lost her concentration for a moment and almost paid dearly with the loss of limb.

The attoh was almost eight-foot-tall, the climb seemed to cast her into a daydream, and then, she heard the welcome sound of drumbeats.

The action began with Adeoha and Sewextu and the six troupe dancers—

accompanied by a lead drummer and a second drummer, and two boys who tapped on an iron gong and shook a set of paired rattles—dancing to the beat of the drums.

The audience looked on at the dancers, but it was Adeoha's movements that drew their attention, her bounding steps, soaring and graceful leaps that seemed to propel her fine form higher and higher, and beyond the glimmering light of the native oil lamps, and for a moment vanishing into the dark of night.

Then she came back in view and descended back to the earth and whirled, taking on the illusion of gliding and floating and nestling the ground beneath her feet, which drew many oohs and aahs from the audience.

Next, Adeoha began to stomp out complex patterns, and her feet beat out a cadence of syncopated rhythms that were unknown to her until that moment. Then she called to the lead drummer with her movements, and he recognized her energy and matched it, then she pushed the drums to new heights.

Now, it was evident to many in the crowd that something was different when she made the motion of chopping firewood, and by her dance and gesture, it seemed the ax had cut her leg, and a child came out of the wound with a gun in hand.

Several people connected her movements, gestures, and rhythms to a specific story, seeing what they had. They were amazed by what they were thinking in their mind's eye, and they began to tell their mates near them that Adeoha's dance somehow caused them to see a tohosu story, the magically endowed water spirits.**

It was then that the joyous mood of the crowd came to an end and a dreadful silence settled as news of the tohosu spread, for the tohosu are the caretakers of the abnormally born and the abnormally aborted, and no ancestral spirit is so feared.

As Adeoha went on with her dance, she pushed her hands through the air toward the sky, then whirled around and spun near the ground, and returned upright again. The large gathering began to see—no, they began to feel—that the dance was a language. And two thousand eyes filled with fear looked on in wonder.

Sewextu was the finest dancer in the province of Allada, and her troupe members were excellent. They kept pace with Adeoha's intricate rhythms with slow and fast, controlled movements, short and quick patterns with an extra beat, and the speed and force of their propulsive arm movements remained graceful and unifying with their spins and leaps while keeping the line fluid—made a fitting and impressive musical accompaniment to the tohosu story.

Scattered here and there among the spectators, people began to speak out, the gist of which: they were saying the story was unfolding in their mind's eye as Adeoha danced each scene out:

The tohosu began to speak as soon as he was born. He told his mother to bring their family together as he wished to talk to them. When they were all assembled, he said, "I have come to hunt. That is why I have come with my gun."

**Dahomean Narrative: A Cross-Cultural Analysis by Melville J. Herskovits & Frances S. Herskovits ~ Enfant Terrible Tales pgs. 256-274

The first day he hunted, he killed an antelope and gave it to his mother to take to the market to sell. At the market were the twins, who are held to have special powers that come from the spirits of the forest. They asked the price of the antelope, but the woman did not want to sell at their price.

"All right," the twins said, "we command the bush," and they told the antelope to run away. So the animal came to life and ran away.

The boy said, "All right. It is nothing." The next day he killed a deer and a buffalo, and his mother took them to market. Again the twins came, and the same thing happened as before.

The boy said, "It is nothing." The next day, he went hunting and came back with many animals. He said, "Today, you will take me with you. But I will remain hidden in your calabash.

When the twins came, they did the same thing as before. The mother refused their offer, so they commanded the animals to run away.

"All right, Mother," the child said, 'let me out.

When the twins saw the child, they were astonished to see a baby standing before them.

The child shook hands with them and said, "Now I have nothing to say to you. But all the animals you have caused to run away must come back here so that my mother may sell them."

At these words, all the animals came back and returned to their previous state, and his mother sold them.

When the twins saw this, they thought, "Ah, he is as terrible as we are."

Slowly, slowly, despite the uneasiness of the spectators, the beauty of Adeoha's dance began to take form and hold them, and the fear they felt eased. Now, everybody there watched her every movement, anxious to see what she would do next.

There was audience participation at every stage in the story, for it is a Dahomean tradition. But a score among the audience told the tale, following along with their own words and movements. From this point on, the audience knew the boy represented Atogon, and the twins represented their rivals from Allada.

The spectators began to give back and have a lot of fun. They laughed and taunted the Allada band whenever the boy got the best of the twins. But, of course, they gave little thought to the cause of it all.

As Adeoha danced, thus began a series of contests of supernatural skills between the boy and the twins.

One of the twins made a mat and caused it to rest in midair. On top of it appeared two bottles of drink, and all three drank there on the mat. The second twin made a needle rise in the air, and the three went and sat on it and ate there.

Not to be outdone by the twins, the child had an enormous pipe, which he lit, and the smoke rose in the air. The three of them climbed up on the smoke and rested there.

When they were about to take leave of each other, the twins suggested that in five days, the child should come and see them. When he went there, the twins gave him a house to rest. And they gave him the food which they had poisoned.

The child spoke to the poison, "Get out of the stew. I want to eat." And the poison obeyed. Later, he looked at his pipe and asked, "Who will watch my sleeping room this evening?"

"I will take care of it," Damballa said.

The next day, everything happened as before, except that evening the child himself watched his sleeping quarter. When the twins came at night to kill him, they saw nothing outside. So they entered the room.

Then they cut the child into pieces and put the pieces in a pot. They cooked it and cooked it from morning till night, but it would not get cooked.

When their father saw this, he was angry and said they did not know how to prepare food. So he sent them to get more wood.

As soon as the twins left, the child came out of the pot and killed their father. He took the skin of the man and covered himself with it.

When the twins returned, they thought the child was their father. He now told them how to prepare the food in the pot—which was their father's body.

So they ate until they came to the head, which they gave to the child—still thinking it was their father—as a mark of respect.

"Now I have killed your father," the child said. Then he took off the skin and escaped. Instantly, the twins were after him.

Now, a river separated the child's country from the country of the twins. When the child was well ahead of them and could not see him, he changed himself into stone.

The twins came to the river. One of them picked up the stone, saying, "If I saw the boy now, I'd kill him with this stone. And he threw it across the river.

When the stone hit the other side, the boy stood up, and he said, "Thank you very much for your company. I am going now."

At this, he returned to his house. His mother said to him, "I did not think you would come home. I thought you were dead."

The child said, "To celebrate, I will kill some game."

From that day on, if he wished to take a journey and asked his mother for permission, she would say, "Good, I have confidence in you."

And with that, the contest ended. The judges declared Allada the winner, for how would it look for the city of Allada to lose to a bush village-like Atogon. But the people-throng declared Atogon, the winner. And they began to rock the night and shout, "Adeoha's name many times."

It was so loud that some of them among the spectators said the distant thunder was Jihossou, the thunder deity. He had heard the commotion and was pleased.

In another quarter of Atogon, Sewextu had prepared platters of food for her troupe and friends to have a feast, the favorites among the people, dishes of antelope, fish, yams, and of course palm wine and millet.

"You must have taken a measure of divining from the bokonon, Sewextu," Adeoha said, "and you must have had a feeling things would go well to have gone ahead and prepared this celebration."

"We did not win," Sewextu said, "but we sent the Alladians' home with their faces of stone."

"We are the victors this year," Dzifa, a member of the troupe, said, "at least in the hearts and minds of the people who were there. And many are saying; they have found a new appeal if they can find how it works."

Sewextu and Adeoha took their party and their good feelings with them to the closing festival dance, where they enjoyed the night away.

###
#####

Adeoha sat there thinking a lot has happened in the last season as she sat under the sacred loko tree. But she had to admit she enjoyed all the attention for a moment but now it was time to move on. Her dance had caused quite a stir among the notables, especially in her grandfathers' clan, to which she belonged.

Now her mind was on her future in the mercantile trade and how quickly could she find another fifteen thousand cowries to add to what she had to establish her new business.

Now, at long last, she could see her friend Sewextu coming up the road. The two friends embraced for a long moment. Then the two of them walked along the path into the forest and sat down at a creek.

"What will you do now?" Sewextu said. "You have danced for the language drums, the children at the storytelling sessions, your mother's gybe, and now you have danced against Allada."

"I think my dancing days are over for now," Adeoha said, "unless you have another mischief in mind," Adeoha said, then laughed. "Seriously though, I look to begin preparation for my mercantile business and the travels it will bring.

"The tohosu story worked out well for the contest, Legba take my breath," Sewextu said. "Only the ancestors could have caused you to go so far from the beaten path."

"What of you, now?" Adeoha said.

"My road has been long, as yours has, Sewextu said.

"I no longer go as much to the language drums because I am called often to Abomey on business.

"I thought that my art was good, "but my time with the society, or perhaps by coincidence as you like to say, it has gotten so much better. I feel I'm in control in ways that I have never known before.

"You have done well," Adeoha said.

"I see things clearer now, Sewextu said. I take my time, and when I do, the words flow."

"And my reward, I see the imagery I have been searching for finding its way into my composition. I have been summoned to Kana by a patron known to be generous as well as a master storyteller—to make new verse for his group's festival.

"That is a master reward," Adeoha said.

"I will see you soon," Sewextu said, and she left there while Adeoha remained. "Well, loko tree," Adeoha thought in humor, "my life is going every which way possible."

The people of Atogon decided to have a public naming ceremony for Adeoha to commemorate her new status. She would be called Gbemende—one who can overcome all obstacles.

Two weeks passed, the rains came, the air was warm, the second harvest began soon, and life returned to its regular round in Da's Belly. At least until the king's house wants thatch [go to war]. And in the moons ahead, we will hear about another people left in desolation, for few Dahomeans get to see the human toll of wars and the slave raids; it's one thing to hear, another to see.

But quietly, there's something else going on, first in small patches here and there, and it took hold in Atogon and then Allada and now throughout the provinces. And now it reaches Abomey, where King Guezo and his army sits. And Adeoha's name is being spoken of by too many Dahomeans for the Royal Court's liking.

The people began to connect Adeoha's dances with the stories of the oracle. And it was taken best by the young people for yesterday they were children, and frolicking beside stories like the oracle and others of magic and mystery.

The myths say the oracle is a place filled with many people, strong friendships, and knowledge about myriad things. And one can find knowledge there, be seen by it, even if not seeking it, or know of its existence.

But soon, Dahomey's peacetime life was disturbed by vague utterances that the King and his court and the nobles were alarmed by Tubutu's great wealth and his daughter's growing army of followers.

Da's Belly's ambitious and envious lords had waited almost twenty years for this opportunity to break Tubutu's house. They had not forgotten that King Guezo had elevated a commoner long absent from Dahomey to nobility.

*****

From the beginning, the King's emissaries and nobles frowned on Tubutu. How quickly the soon-to-be King gave Tubutu an audience on his arrival in Da's Belly. The ease he gave money to Guezo's campaign to seize the throne from his half-brother and his display of bravery during the conflict. But, with that, he established the King's favor.

And you could see their noble blood hot with envy when King Guezo stood before the palace while the crowd shouted out, make Tubutu a provincial chief or caboceer and raise him to noble status.

Those who were seeking Tubutu's demise were already plotting to mock Tubutu in the eyes of the King. They had devised a plan that some of the duties and taxes would disappear. Then, as gobunuga, the loss would fall upon his head or worse. But the scheme did not go as planned because Tubutu gainsaid the King, which left the lord's speechless.

The nobles reasoned that Tubutu got away with his folly because Guezo was young and new to the throne, and he hadn't had the time to consider his power was absolute. And they could not mention this flagrant disrespect to his sovereignty, that one of his subjects refused a great honor, for one does not annoy a king with unpleasant remembrances.

But that took place some twenty seasons ago. Since then, Tubutu has spent much effort and time trying to keep out of harm's way and diverting attention from himself. Now, Adeoha's sudden rise to popularity across the provinces has given the nobles a chance they have long-awaited.

It was such a grave matter that Ajatauvi, the clan head, called a council meeting to discuss it on this very day.

As Adeoha looked about Ajatauvi's palatial compound, she wondered how her little dance could threaten the lives of so many people. On one side of the court, she sat beside her mother, Lady Lamtaala, aunt Lady Owusua, and grandmother Lady

Glyya. And several other notable women of the clan.

About the square sat Lord Ewansi, O'Gwumike, and Lord Tubutu. Also present, a short distance away, sat a row of elders, heads of the various guilds and crafts. And inside the square sat Ajatauvi.

The venerable head of the Xenu Awansuju, Owner Of A Mountain People, stood and looked at the assembled members and the invited women's council. Then, he addressed the sib members and allotted time for those wishing to speak, and he listened.

"Lord Ewansi should have watched her more closely," a woman said." She is always getting into trouble and speaking in rebellious tones."

"She should not have been allowed to join the cult of the Language of the Drums," another woman hollered out. "They are trouble makers. We fought many wars against their forefathers, and only in the last few generations have we let them back among us."

"I remind those present from the council of women," Ajatauvi said, "you have no standing here. You were invited as a courtesy."

The Sib members knew that some people in high places whispered a plot by Tubutu to cease the throne and abetted by his daughter's popularity among her large following.

"It seems to me, great chief," an elderly member of the clan said, "whoever is spreading this deception, and it could be anyone who has an ax to grind. If this talk should continue, our businesses throughout the kingdom could be damaged."

Adeoha's acceptance by the Language of the Drums brought to light that both Adeoha and Tubutu were of the families of the ancient ancestral clans—Mami, Hevioso, Aholu, Loko. And others—who were at constant war with the Dahomean kings over the throne.

"It is true, Ajatauvi said, we the people of the leopard once held great contempt for the Mami and the serpent followers. But let us not forget that our rulers sent many of their priests and people into slavery during the days of the conflict.

"But it was in the long past in the time of King Agaja and King Tegbesa. Now we all live together here in peace, and their Dangbe worship has grown strong in our Foy [Fon] tradition.

"We are a clan of high status and many personages with strong names. We have demonstrated our loyalty to the Aladahonu kings since the Dakou, the first Aladahonu king. His Majesty King Guezo should consider this, but one never knows what to expect.

"On the other side of the coin, the house of Lord Tubutu is now paddling their vessels in dangerous seas, it is small, and the king's memory of it is small."

"Have I," Tubutu said, "the great xenuga and venerable elders, "your permission to speak before this esteemed body."

"Of course, Lord Tubutu," Ajatauvi said.

"These untruths reach beyond Adeoha and me and your respected clan," Tubutu said. "By its very nature, it can bring great harm and disruption to the lives of all the people of Dahomey. I want to assure this assembled body that the truth will rear its head."

Adeoha wondered as her father spoke, how can he prove these accusations false. He cannot say with any certainty from where they came.

CHAPTER NINE

As Adeoha went home, the rains fell gently; she changed and set out for the village court to meet her three most important friends. As she looked beyond the marketplace, she could see them just as the rain began to fall harder. The four of them ran for cover under a nearby anya tree.

Later, when the rain stopped, the friends went their separate ways, and Adeoha had an impulse to visit the loko tree on one of O'Gwumike's fields. She went there sometime when she wanted to clear her head and think.

"The chatter is baseless and the rumors ugly about father mine and me together in some plot to cease power," Adeoha thought.

As Adeoha walked, she heard footsteps coming up behind her. "I will come with you," Sewextu said. "No matter," Adeoha said, "I will come to meet with you later."

Adeoha ran the winding path under the silk-cotton trees. She saw the ebbing sunlight gleaming through the leaves. The patches of red, blue sky sparkled in the trees of the same hue.

As she ran the winding path, it turned straight. Now she could see people of all ages stop what they were doing and line the direction she ran. They shouted her name as she passed them, and it was the same all along her way.

After reaching her destination, she sat down reeling with weariness and emotion and leaned back against the trunk of the loko tree. "I have made things worse with my run," she thought. "What they say about it today will be different tomorrow.

As she sat there thinking, she looked to the sky. The last thing she saw was a thick, cloudy blue mist descend from the sky. She was too tired to be surprised and fell into a deep dream as the cloud enveloped her. And it lifted her once again amid the happy days of childhood.

It was the hottest night ever, and the other children chose Sewextu to lead the riddling and proverb session, which preceded the storytelling. Sewextu looked at her and said something about 'naked going out and now covered with cloth.' But Adeoha had no answer because she wasn't listening, for her mind was elsewhere: Where in the village are the boy's meeting?

"The answer is corn," Kemi shouted out before anyone else could. She was quite pleased with herself and went on to answer the coming riddles as fast as Sewextu spoke them, for riddling is a rapid thing.

"What excuse can I give that will allow me to take leave of here, now?" Adeoha thought. Sewextu's words provided an answer. "We'll take a break now instead of going straight into the stories, Sewextu said.

"There is a special reason for our departure from what is customary. The Lady Ohema Owusua will grace us with her presence." There were gasps all around prompted by her high esteem as a storyteller and creator of verse.

"Adeoha quietly eased away from her friends without being noticed. It was not a day of any particular celebration or feast, but everywhere, people young and old were having a good time, and the drummers and musicians were about, and it was as festive a day as any she could remember.

As Adeoha searched for the boy's meeting place, she almost walked upon a group of elders sitting in a semicircle about a baobab tree. She kneeled, looking around her for the boy's meeting place. Then she gazed upon the men, seven in all.

She could tell by their manner they were men of high status. They dressed in princely togas of earth colors, and they wore bracelets of silver and bronze upon their wrists and ankles, their sandals ornamented, two wore chiefs' hats, and two others had circlets of silver around their heads.

Adeoha smiled that the men had no trouble filling their calabashes with whatever was in the large flask near them and inhaling smoke from long, wood-carved pipes while amusing themselves with their discourse.

Now Adeoha's curiosity got the best of her. She intended to listen in on their words for only a moment and then find the hut where the boys were meeting, for it had to be nearby. But because of the noise from the festivities, she could not hear them.

Suppose I could somehow get to the baobab tree where they sit without them seeing me. Then, I'll be in a good place to hear their words without being seen.

Perched on a branch high atop the baobab tree was a Wututu bird singing. The Wututu called Adeoha to come to the tree. Without thought, her body inclined on the ground and slithered through the moonlit clearing and came to rest at the side of the baobab tree.

"The venerable Erkua," Nnewanu said, "has raised this our first meeting after many years to an exalted status by stating the presence of the sacred rainbow serpent, Damballa."

"Yes, I did see a python in the light of the clearing," Erkua said, pointing, "it was right over there, and then it curled around the tree and disappeared."

"And what has this humble body of men done to merit such an honor as a visit from the sacred python," Yaifa asked.

"Perhaps it is the millet whiskey we drink," Nnewanu said, "that should be held responsible for what Erkua has seen," And much laughter filled them.

"Or maybe it is the presence of the most esteemed Eldeide, the diviner of kings," Nnewanu said.

"What have you to say to all this, Eldeide," Omaewe asked, "after your absence from among us for so many years? And they raised their calabashes to him in respect.

"My years of study," Eldeide said, "may reveal that of all the tales told to us as children, it may be the most unlikely one that will carry the answer of a given time, the story of the oracle," which brought forth laughter from the body of men.

"According to the ancient myth," Eldeide said. "It is not only a place where magic abounds in the everyday lives of its people. It is also where there is hidden knowledge for all who seek it."

Adeoha listened wonderingly on two accounts: first, she was astonished to come upon the distinguished Eldeide, widely known as the greatest bokonon in all Dahomey. She had heard his stories all too well, how he had great riches and attention while still a stripling, and his preeminence was all the more notable because it occurred during the troubled reign of King Adandozan.

They say that when Eldeide read the du [the signs within the divination system of Fa], he did not oblige his wealthy patrons with favorable utterances—he told them only what he divined. It was so, even with King Adandozan, which could have cost him his life. But he was called from his opulent lifestyle by the ancient Yeveh Vodun ancestors to study the ancient prophecies. So he answered that call and since then has given his life to scholarly pursuits.

Adeoha was also surprised that such a prominent personage as Eldeide would place importance on the story of the oracle.

"I have divined," Eldeide said, "that the oracle may have more to do with the gods than man."

"Then it is no concern of ours," Senanu said, speaking for the first time.

"Anything that has to do with the gods to some extent involves humans," Eldeide said.

"If Eldeide's divination adds to human knowledge, it could be of value in my profession," Awegbe, the great azondato [sorcerer], said. "I wait to hear your learned words, honorable Eldeide. But before you begin, I have a question. I saw you recently addressing a number of our young people, and I am curious to what point you were trying to make."

"I was telling our future warriors, Eldeide said, at this precise time in their lives, they are no longer children but not yet adults. I was trying to convey that many challenges lie in wait for them. Their lives need not be simple or fixed. Fate is not unchangeable. There are solutions.

"They must learn to recognize the lessons of the crossroads, for these are oracular moments in time, where doors open and close to their Destiny. And they must ask the ancestors for guidance, for they have walked the earth and experienced the same problems. It could be a strong wind or another vessel that changes one's direction and down another road. That is the gist of my meaning, Awegbe."

"Honorable elders, Eldeide continued, "I know that each of you is well aware of the fa tales I am about to offer to you for discourse. I ask you to consider two myths, the first from a Legba tale and a Fa tale of divination.

"What is important here is that the first story sets the precedent of Legba consulting with an oracle:

"Mawou tells her children to come before her to find out who will receive Ashe [so be it] and become the next most powerful. Each of Legba's brothers brings a huge sacrifice. But Legba consults the oracle before he comes, and he finds that all he has to bring is a bright red feather set upright on his forehead.

"When Mawou sees this, she grants Legba the power of Ashe because he has shown he understands the power of information and is unwilling to carry burdens."

"In the second story," Eldeide went on, "when Legba walked the earth among men, he had much knowledge as the maker of magic charms and was the first to make them. One day Legba met a man called Awe, and he began to make magic charms for him. If someone needed one, they came to Awe, and both good and bad charms spread across the land.

"Mawou became angry. She called Legba to the sky and said to him, 'if people cannot see you, you cannot do this again.' So Legba was rendered invisible, and he could no longer walk the earth among people."

"This brings me to the Fa tale of divination, Eldeide said. Fa is personified in the myth of Gbadu. Mawou told Gbadu to live atop a palm tree in the sky and observe the kingdoms of the Earth, the Sky, and the Sea.

"In time, Legba told Mawou there was a great war on earth, a great war in the sky, and a great war in the sea, and if it were not for Gabadu, these three kingdoms would soon be destroyed since the people did not know how to behave. Legba told Mawou it would be good to send Gbadu to earth. 'No.' Mawou said. 'Let Gbadu remain in the sky.'"

"I pondered these stories for the longest, Eldeide said. I wondered why the Vodu had chosen them and to what end. It was then a new knowledge of divination came to my head. And surprisingly, and to my astonishment, it was beyond the fate of Dahomey. It was about the Destiny of man and the earth.

"I have, as we all here know, divine in the house with sixteen doors. And each door has sixteen places around the world."

"That's a lot of places you diviners have to go in and out of," Erkua said, which drew amused chuckles among the elders.

"One day, while I was in a magical interlude, Eldeide said. I threw the kernels, read the du off my board, and a seventeenth house appeared with sixteen doors, but each door had one place instead of sixteen.

But I was astounded, for it was the first house outside the system. And the du showed the first door had the keys of the future that Mawou gave to Gbadu. What will the other fifteen doors tell? Perhaps another realm of divination to comprehend.

"Then a second door opened, I was able to see Sakpata, Sogbo, Agbe, and Age, four of the seven children of Mawou.

"Now Mawou had given Legba the work of visiting all the kingdoms ruled by his brothers and giving an account of what was happing there. Thus, Legba knows the languages of his brothers, and he is the only one who knows the language of Mawou. If one of his brothers wishes to speak to Mawou, he must give the message to Legba. All beings, humans, and gods—must address themselves to Legba before they can approach Mawou-Lissa.

"Legba is the linguist for his brothers before Mawou. So they all began to speak at once and state their grievances which Legba told to Mawou—human activity on earth, the sky, and the sea has gotten much worse and threatened to destroy their kingdoms. And they blamed Legba and Gbadu, for they were given charge of watching human beings and reporting what they saw to Mawou.

"Sakpata said, 'A myriad of the life-sustaining species that Mawou created to protect and advance life on earth was no more, and those remaining were rapidly vanishing.'

"Sogbo said, 'I can no longer guard those below. Men fight and quarrel and plunder the world. The fire on earth is so great the smoke will reach the sky, destroying the heavens.'

"Agbe said, 'The fish and birds that dwell with the sea can no longer find their places and are dying out because of human folly.'

"Age said, 'Where are the lions, the tigers, the wolves, the elephants, and the bees? I can no longer see them. Human activity is causing the bush to fill with smoke, and soon no rain will fall, and the heat will dry the earth, and the trees and all else will burn.'

"These times are difficult," Mawou said.

"Let me visit the earth," Legba said. "Let me go and find out the true nature of men. Let me find out if all men are accomplices in the continued destruction of life and the earth, or, if only some men are involved, then why are they not in command."

"Legba's brothers shrilled in disbelief at what Legba was asking. Then, they let it be known that Mawou had made Legba invisible and could not revoke this."

"But Legba had consulted the oracle, and he knew that all he needed to do was find a magical oracle on earth which would contain hidden knowledge of his task. So Legba made the case before Mawou that he would walk the land among the people in human form with no knowledge or memory of himself or the sky, which would remain until he returned before Mawou.

"Thus, Mawou decreed that Legba would go to earth and have no memory of the sky and would be born and raised in human form to learn what he could about humans and their ways. He would bring this knowledge back to the sky, and Mawou would decide.

"Then a third door opened, and the du showed even this could not have happened if not for Mawou's love for her spoiled, youngest son. She seldom involves herself in the trappings of man, but she had to do something, as little as it was, to help Legba's human form find his way.

"Please, pardon me," Nnewanu said. "Our calabashes need more millet for our thirst. I want to enjoy your heho [parable, or fable]. I have heard nothing like it before.

"I look forward to hearing the rest of it," Awegbe said. "Knowing these things can be worth a lot of cowries; people are always in need of information about something or other."

"So Mawou brought him to her bosom in the sky and revealed to Legba's human form all things. But he would remember none of it, his only recollection of the event was what had happened at the edge of the universe when he spoke the words— 'I have the answer.'

"Then he went back and forth for a moment with his thoughts, for only his mind was there, for his body was back on earth engaged in conversation with another person, for it all happened in a heartbeat. But as the years went by, he began to wonder if he had been someplace else before awakening at the edge of the universe.

"But Mawou knew to give to Legba's human form the instincts of the sky, an aura, an indelible influence; for she knows he will never believe who he is, what human person would. But he has to consider it unless he will not do the work necessary to complete his task.

"Mawou also spoke the language of the sky to four people (two were yovo, and two were black, of whom two are young and two are elderly), who would meet Legba's human form during their lives. Mawou embedded in each of them, at four oracular appointed moments during his life, what they would say to him: 'You're God,' or, 'You look like God.'

"Of course, Legba's human form has no Idea of what's going on, and for many years, only occasionally would he think about his awakening at the edge of the universe. But it left him wondering what power commanded what happened in the sky and the four people who spoke to him without remembering.

"As I opened each door, I traveled through time and the world. But one of the doors I opened in the du was a place in the future. I think it is the oracle. And there, the onus was on Legba's human form to make the magic, not the gods.

"And there's a spiritual realm at work there, the deities, nature, the ancestors, and these forces push him to take on the impossible when it comes. So he opens the road to his fa by recognizing the magical engravings of his surroundings, and importantly he realizes the magic was there before he came.

"But it is the people of the oracle who seize Legba's human form and push him beyond human conception. And from there, he will be fixed on his Destiny with the help of the mystical laws of the universe and the workings of cause and effect, and by the guidance of the ancestors and nature's spirits commanded into existence by Mawou.

"Well, I have shared with you my divination and thoughts, which will hold you until our next meeting. However, I think the oracle story is more of the bwenoho kind than heho, for it is our true history, and the oracular place has stood through the echoes of time."

"This has been some great entertainment, a good time for us all on the highest level," Nnewanu said. "We are gladdened to see you, Eldeide, the bokonoe turned storyteller," and everyone laughed, none more than Eldeide.

At that moment, Adeoha awakened. It took her a while to gather her three souls to her. While she sat there thinking about the dream she just had, she could see someone coming toward her in the moonlight. Then she recognized the face of Hwesbadja, a tenant farmer on one of her grandfather's estates.

Adeoha had shared a good friendship with Hwesbadja's son Kakpole, who died in one of King Guezo's wars. Hwesbadja found joy as they reminisced about their moments with Kakpole. Soon she gave the old man a loving hug and headed home.

When Adeoha reached Tubutu's compound, she hurried through the gate and went home to find Lamtaala waiting.

"They are already saying an army of people flocked to see you and cheered as you ran," Lamtaala said. "It's not something the king will take pleasure in hearing."

"It just happened, Mother," Adeoha said, remembering those were Sewextu's very words to her when she put her name before the language drums society."

"It seems there's always political overtones in what you do. I know you don't mean it that way. Your father is waiting for you." Lamtaala said

"Forgive me, Father, for the distress I have caused," Adeoha said. "If it were not for my dance—" before she could finish, her father reached out and pulled her to him gently.

"It is not you that has brought the trouble," Tubutu said. " And you have accomplished a lot that gives Lamtaala and I pride."

"One thing has led to another," Adeoha said.

"The run today just brought it to a head," Tubutu said. "I have heard, their words are well-chosen: that you have an army of followers. You have not slept, so go and get a little rest.

Going from her father's house, Adeoha prayed quietly within her heart, "help us, Minona, Goddess of women."

At that moment, in another district of Atogon, a conversation was taking place regarding the same matter. "The time has come for us to leave Da's Belly," Mautusan said.

"What are you saying, Mautusan?" Patricia asked.

"What has happened to change things so fast," Robert said.

Mautusan looked about him cautiously and began to speak softly, "It is no longer safe for us here. Lady Adeoha is drawing too much attention, and that alone is not good in Da's Belly, and now there are rumors that Tubutu is planning to cease Guezo's throne.

"This is serious," Robert said.

"Today, as soon as we have gathered our things, and we still have the light of day, or tomorrow before light," Mautusan said. "I have worked out the route we will take.

"We have to see Adeoha; hopefully, we can find her in the short time we have," Patricia said.

"We will find her," Robert said.

"We learn to live in these moments," Mautusan said. "Why something is believed or not has more to do with the power behind it than truth or reason."

"Go now with haste," Mautusan said. "I will send Oluwole with you, and when you return, gather your things; we will leave as soon as we can.

"How much time do we have," Robert said, "where minutes matter in our leaving."

"If the Half Heads come for Adeoha and Tubutu," Mautusan said, "they will probably come for you too because of your friendship because whoever has the King's ear would profit.

"If the King finds out about you, you will be guests at the palace and not able to leave until he tires of your English."

An hour later, Robert and Patricia stood at the entrance to Tubutu's compound and quickly walked to Lamtaala's house, where they found Adeoha.

"What I'm about to say is in secrecy," Robert said, "Mautusan has said it must be so."

"We will leave before nightfall or early in the morning," Patricia said. "What will you do.

"My father and others are doing what they can," Adeoha said.

"I know we must go, but it's hard to leave like this," Patricia said.

"Things will work out. Now you are beginning your journey home a season earlier," Adeoha said. "There are always two sides to the coin.

You aren't prepared for a fight, Adeoha. Anything can happen," Robert said.

"I would like to see my friends safely away from here," Adeoha said as she embraced her two friends and pushed them off.

At that moment, in Abomey, King Guezo and his Royal Court were in session. Four hundred of the most important officials in the realm looked on: the migan and meu, commander and chiefs of the army, the gbonuga or caboceers, the yovoga, and the male and female generals of the two brigades of the Dahomean army.

"What is said may or may not be true," Guezo said, "but it is not without possibility. Tubutu has wealth and powerful clans around him, and his daughter Adeoha has amassed a large following, which the court cannot overlook."

"What are the words of your royal ancestors," the meu said. "You must crush an ant that troubles you, or it becomes an elephant." So then, it was decided the Half Heads, Dahomey's greatest warriors would be sent at once to Atogon. Tubutu and Adeoha would be brought to Abomey and detained in the palace until called before the royal court.

*****

Tubutu sat before his bungalow and pondered the burden he carried: "The Aladahonu Kings are quick to strike when someone makes too big a show, Tubutu thought. So the King has to end the talk quickly, unless he appears weak before his subjects, and invites more plots against his person.

"Even if Adeoha left Dahomey and went to another country, it would not save

Adeoha or the situation we find ourselves. The King could send the Half Heads to get her first friend Sewextu and bring her to Abomey, often a ploy of past Aladahonu kings, knowing the person sought would give up to save their first friend; something Adeoha would do without hesitation.

"If Adeoha remains in Dahomey, Guezo can punish her by bestowing some great honor on her, like a marriage with one of the princes or the king himself. Or consign her to the Ahosi Corps, or send her into slavery."

Tubutu's quandary, knowing not, he jumped up and walked to Lamtaala's house, for she was always astute when needed

"I am not in fear for myself or my people or your father's clan," Tubutu said. "We have all been through times like these. Adeoha is a different matter."

"Whether Adeoha leaves Dahomey or not," Lamtaala said, "only one outcome is certain."

"In the name of Legba, there must be a way we can save our daughter," Tubutu said.

Suddenly, an idea came to Lamtaala's head, and a ray of hope was heard in her voice as she spoke. "There's something about this—that may connect with the language drums—and Eldeide the bokonoe may have an answer."

"I'm not keen on diviners, too many things can influence them, but he is well respected. I will find him," Tubutu said.

*****

As Eldeide milled about outside his hut, he listened with a keen ear to the sounds of the earth as a new day awoke. Then, he began to walk through the very thick part of the forest where he kept his diving instruments. His shrine was also located there, unknown to anyone except the few who had visited him there. Once he reached it, a cluster of silk cotton, loko, and anya trees shrubs he had found. He sat and began thinking.

He recalled the times he studied the structure of the heavens and the movements of the stars. But once he was within the power of the seventeenth house (which brings up Adeoha's dream). He saw in another door a heavenly body called a grand throng gleaned from his studies. Then he was surprised that a second grand throng would appear in the sky during the time of the oracle.

When Tubutu arrived at the village near Eldeide's home, he was told a villager would guide him there in the forest and have his consent to receive you.

It was not a long wait before Tubutu stood in the presence of Eldeide, who was tall and lean, with a big bush of white hair that sat high atop his head, and he possessed a warm smile which calmed Tubutu and put him at ease. Tubutu bowed low and reverently before him and introduced himself, and spoke, "I have heard the stories of your spiritual insight and what it portends for all men. I am honored to be in your presence."

"Come and sit with me, my son; it is not often I have visitors," Eldeide said. "What matter has brought you among us?"

"I look for some sharing of your wisdom in a matter before my house," Tubutu said. "I have a trouble that will take a miracle to resolve.

"Then it is a miracle you seek," Eldeide said. "Do you believe in miracles, my son? "Fa has dominion over destiny, but Legba has mastery over destiny's paths, skirting through the lines of fate and widening and narrowing the pathways. Perhaps this is what's going on now.

Tubutu looked at the diviner, somewhat bewildered. Was the great bokonoe saying that Legba had something to do with all that has happened.

"I have cast the magic lots," Eldeide said, "for I am familiar with all that you have told me, and the configuration of lines show a time when the children of your daughter's children will walk on the land of the oracle."

"Now," Tubutu thought, "he talks of the oracle, a children's tale as the answer to the seriousness of my problem."

"This is what I have divined," Eldeide said. "You have your answer to all things that brought you before me. Perhaps you being here is a sign, and tomorrow I will go among the people and speak about the oracle's prophecy and Adeoha's journey.

"Thank you," Tubutu said, and he bowed low and took his leave.

As Tubutu walked toward his compound, he gathered his thoughts and reasoned that Eldeide's words were good ones. "It matters little whether I believe the old oracle story or not, as long as Eldeide proclaims it so, and that Adeoha is under the sign of the oracle, and her time with the language drums has deemed it so.

"The words of Eldeide will have force, Tubutu thought, but they will make Adeoha even more of a threat to the King unless she is beyond his reach. But the diviner has provided a way for Adeoha to leave Dahomey without causing anyone harm. She would be going on a spiritual journey and not for political reasons.

"But if the Half Heads find her first, then nothing has changed, and we are all lost. Time is needed for Eldeide's words to take effect and a new discourse to begin.

Tubutu found Adeoha having fun and playing with Oshun and her brothers and sisters of a different mother. "Daughter mine, I have just come from seeing Eldeide. Maybe he has given us a way out. But we have to move with the speed and the cunning of the leopard."

Adeoha thought of her dream when she heard the diviner's name. And Tubutu told her what Eldeide had said.

"Is there no way to save my days in Dahomey," Adeoha asked?

"I think not," Tubutu said, "unless you want to wed a prince or a king." His words were meant to ease the situation, and Adeoha smiled as best she could.

"I wish to say goodbye to Sewextu, but she's in Ajajou.

"Just as well, there's no time," Tubutu said. "I feel the Half Heads are not far. If they arrive before we leave, there we no choice but to go with them."

"I understand, Father," Adeoha said.

"While I am gone, gather the things you will need and ready to go when I return," Tubutu said."

"In the name of Legba," Tubutu thought as he left his compound. "Let me find Mautusan."

Tubutu counted on getting Adeoha out of Dahomey, where she would no longer pose a threat to the King. And Eldeide, by what Eldeide says when he addresses his followers, should lay to rest the intrigues of a plot to seize the royal stool. And leave the King without need for retaliation, and hopefully, things can return as before.

Adeoha cringed at the thought of leaving her family and country. "But it will be a small price to pay," she thought, "if it means peace in Dahomey."

And has Adeoha gathered her things, She lamented her fate, and called out to Fa, "Life has taken me this way and that, cover me with clay, so that I may be hidden, and the King and his men cannot find me."

CHAPTER TEN

Tubutu ran fast, for many lives were at risk, and soon he was there, and he could see Mautusan. So his plan to leave Adeoha with Mautusan went with reason. Besides, it's the only plan given the short notice.

It was a good one because Mautusan came to Dahomey from a distant land, and he was probably returning by the same route, so he must know the land, and how to circumvent danger, at least that's what he hoped; for in truth, he knew little about him, they did not walk in the same circles.

"Hello, my friend," Mautusan said, "I would be glad to see you if not for the occasion. I can guess why you are here."

"I have come for the same reason you are leaving and with the same urgency," Tubutu said. "I ask you to wait and take Adeoha with you."

"I think it will be safer if I leave now, Mautusan said. "I have to think of the yovos. I want to get them back where they started from without having to pay a visit to see the King."

"You're right; the sooner you're out of Dahomey, the better," Tubutu said.

"Robert and Patricia have already left with Gbwe and await me at a hidden place not far," Mautusan said.

"There must be a way," Tubutu said.

"Why have you not brought Adeoha with you," Mautusan said.

"I was not sure you would be here, and there is another matter I have to attend to with Adeoha," Tubutu said.

"If you can reach Glidji, I can wait for you there. I will take three days to get there," Mautusan said.

"I have kin in Glidji, among the Guin," Tubutu said.

"I will meet you to the west of the big lake, and I'll leave Tehseloh with you," Mautusan said.

"I'm okay," Tubutu said. "You need your people."

"I have to leave him with you. You know the sea lanes, but you don't know the marshes where we will be, and you will not be able to find us without him, Mautusan said.

"I have been doing business in the towns along the ocean's coast a long time. Tehseloh can provide you with safe passage to Glidji. Where will you go now?" Mautusan said.

"Based on what you have told me, I go now to get Adeoha, and from there we go to Lake Aheme," Tubutu said.

"Ahh, that is good. Tehseloh knows the country, a day's journey from Lake Aheme; you will be at the entrance to the marsh country and the Popo kingdom. I will instruct Gbwe to meet you there with one of my longboats. Tehseloh knows where."

"Then it is set, Adeoha, and I will see you in Glidji," Tubutu said.

"Just practice unusual caution. You don't want to take your boat into a warlike tribe or stopped by a British man-of-war. Add to that Portuguese and Spanish slavers because the British have increased patrols and watch the ports."

"I'll leave now; where is your man Tehseloh," Tubutu said.

"I sent him on task with my leaving," Mautusan said.

"How have you come so familiar with this region," Tubutu said.

"During my youth, I played in the marshes with my friends among the Peda people. Later, when I was running from the King, they sheltered me.

"This is my first time hearing of this. I suspected you were a seaman, and something was going on with you—but your involvement with the yovos and theirs with Adeoha was good—so it didn't concern me," Tubutu said.

"I have found in the lagoons little known outlets and inlets to and from the sea that I have benefited from over the years," Mautusan said.

Tubutu's eyebrows raised in surprise as he heard about Mautusan's sea merchant business. It offered means and protection for Adeoha if she remained in Afrika.

"I have heard things about you. You returned to Dahomey after a long absence having amassed great riches, Guezo made you a noble, and you married high," Mautusan said.

It was then Tehseloh returned. And in moments, Tubutu and Mautusan were off, So they began their separate ways, planning to wind up together again in three days.

*****

"Let us go to the creek, daughter mine. I know it's been a tiring day, the way you have given yourself over to Oshun and

Tubutu's sons and daughters. I know you are close to them," Lamtaala said.

There they sat down beside a steep rocky hill listening to the cascading stream and the Wututu singing their stories. And they listened, perhaps hearing and visualizing conversations they had together that seemed like only yesterday. When they made their way through the conclave in laughter, it was often about life and things.

"What will you do without me, Mother? You will be free of my buzzing about you like a bee for ways to get me out of some trouble I alone caused," Adeoha said.

"First, it was the language of the drums, then your dance of anticipation, and now your dance against Allada. Perhaps these things are more than coincidence, Lamtaala said.

"Regardless, you must live life for you, face your trials from where they come. You will have your way; You are on a good road." Then they headed back home.

"Mother, tell Sewextu I said goodbye, and I will miss our days together, and I know she's going to have success in Abomey as big as a baobab tree," Adeoha said.

As Lamtaala and Adeoha passed through the compound's gate, they could hear Tubutu calling his retainers.

A moment later, Oluwole and Tokou were kneeling before Tubutu. "Yes, your highness," they said.

"The urgent matter is now before us. Prepare to leave," Tubutu said, turning to see Adeoha coming with Gaye and Tsawi at her side.

"Father mine, we have talked about freeing Gaye and Tsawi before. They have pleased me very much. They were with me through all the rounds of my new business. I wish you to reward them with their freedom and cowries enough to start a new life," Adeoha said."

Tubutu thought, and he granted Adeoha her wish.

Out in the courtyard, Adeoha saw Oshun and her half-siblings waiting together for one last goodbye though she had already spent the better part of the day with them. She hugged each one of them tight, but one among them took her leaving hard.

"They say you will leave us and go someplace far away, and I will never see you again," said the misty-eyed little girl half the seasons [in age] of Adeoha.

"I will miss the things we did together," Adeoha said and hugged her.

Next, Oshun, O'Gwumike, and Lady Glyya held Adeoha as long as possible and bade her farewell with their last sayings.

Tubutu, Adeoha, and the three left there and headed east to a boathouse near the beginning of the lama marsh. They met a trusted boatman there and bought two strong boats for their continued journey southeast to the sea coast.

"I would not have expected you to go forth in these swamps and marshes as well as you have," Tehseloh said to Tubutu.

"I owe it to my days before coming to Dahomey," Tubutu said.

"I now feel confident you can lead us to Gbwe and then to Mautusan. Mautusan thinks you can rescue your daughter and find him unless he would not have sent me with you. He knows how dangerous the marshes are in Popoe land," Tehseloh said.

"I'll take the first watch, get some sleep, "I'll come and get you," Tubutu said. Then Tehseloh joined Adeoha and the rest of the band in the land of sleep.

The next day, they reached Lake Aheme and settled in; Tubutu and Tokou took the boat out on the lake. Adeoha, Oluwole, and Tehseloh stayed ashore. As spectacular as the view from the shore, they did not notice the dead loko tree partially submerged in the water until the canoe stopped.

Then Tubutu dove into the water, brought up a chest, and dove again and brought up a second chest. He returned to shore and emptied the contents into four leather pouches. After that, Tubutu and his party left there, and they went to a place not far away and rested the night.

Tubutu told Adeoha that you now possess great wealth, but you should not show too much pride and wish to keep your gold and wealth. You must put it in a canoe and hide it under the water as I have, for men cannot be trusted.

"Thank you, Father mine. I will remember what you have done today and what you have told me," Adeoha said.

At dawn the next day, Tubutu set out on a day and a half journey to Popoe country and meet Gbwe. As they got nearer to the marshes, they began to experience sicknesses, and they grew tired. Adeoha told them to paddle slowly, and in time she gathered plants and fruits growing near the water. She mixed them for drinking and rubbing, and it invigorated them.

Finally, they reached the marshes and found Gbwe and two Kroomen. Tubutu's longboats were double-banked for two or four rowers. Tubutu decided to leave Oluwole and Tokou at the entrance to the marsh—which put smiles on their faces looking at the women in the village—with friends of Tehseloh until he returned.

Thus began their travels to find Mautusan and bring Adeoha under his protection until they reached the distant shores of Cape Palmas. Tehseloh and Gbwe guided the vessel's course through the strong currents of the intersecting rivers at the entrance to the islands and towns near Lome, where Mautusan was now waiting.

As they neared a river flowing to the sea, they knew crossing it to the other side would take them to where they were to meet Mautusan. As they approached the inlet, they were startled by the shill sound of many voices. They could see many canoes and a coffle of fifty slaves or more coming through the marshland toward them.

They concealed themselves, and the longboats in the high grass, out of sight of the armed men and the coffle of slaves moving through the water lanes on both sides of them, not looking to see and hardly breathing.

Slowly, the sounds of the slavers and their human cargo grew silent, but they did not dare move until more time had passed, for they could not be sure if there were more of their party, for they were known to travel in that fashion. Later, Tubutu felt the danger was done, and everyone breathed a sigh of relief. And by day's end, they found their way to Mautusan.

Well, all is well, now that you and Lady Adeoha have arrived. But you must return to an uncertain outcome, Tubutu," Mautusan said.

"As soon as I can, kings can easily be misled when the tide turns against them," Tubutu said. But enough has happened that I should feel my family is safe, and things are well in Da's Belly.

Patricia and Robert were beside themselves with joy to see Adeoha again. They embraced all around.

"We arrived yesterday, it took us two days, through all sorts of twists and turns, stoppings and goings, avoiding this and avoiding that, but it was an experience, traveling and feeling yet other parts of Afrika," Patricia said.

"Then Mautusan told us you were joining us if all went well, and now we leave for Cape Palmas. An awful lot has happened in two days," Robert said.

"We have all had our moments getting here," Adeoha said. Just then, a Kroomen came to Adeoha with a message from her father.

"I was about to join my father, but the message I just received asks you to join us, and Mautusan is with him," Adeoha said.

There they were, the five of them, Adeoha and Tubutu, Robert and Patricia, and Mautusan, far away from their homes, surrounded by swamps and marshes and wild coastal town in another country.

"I have four pouches here before me, Tubutu said. "The two pouches are

Adeoha's to start her life anew in Afrika or America; the choice is hers. They are then turning to Robert and Patricia. These two pouches are given to you whether or not Adeoha comes to America.

"They will bring great wealth and provide you with higher status in your country than before, which I hope will prosper whatever is needed to council and protect Adeoha if she comes to your country.

"Then she is your daughter by your inheritance of these two pouches, and she inherits from you the knowledge of the legalisms and customs and taboos of your country and your advice on what can be done or not done if she wants to venture down new roads or falls into harm's way.

"And to Mautusan, who we all owe a debt of gratitude that will always be remembered. The fates seem to have put us all in his hands at one time or another. I would have given him many pouches of gold and silver for what he has done. I have gathered from our talks the kind of person he is, and it would have been an insult to offer him money—as I would have been.

"Then Tubutu asked everyone's leave to spend the last moments with Adeoha before leaving. While Mautusan had the two Kroomen who came with Tubutu, and two other Kroomen, take him to where Oluwole and Tokou were waiting.

Tubutu and Adeoha embraced for what they both knew was probably the last time. And then their eyes fixed, and in his head, he thanked Mawou for her safety to this point in her life and asked to keep her safe in the days yet to come.

Once, the Kroomen returned with word that Tubutu had found his men, and they had departed for Dahomey safely. It was the signal to Mautusan to begin the sea voyage that would take them through the dangerous inlets and unsuspecting currents within the overture of the gold and ivory coasts, as his friend Dinocencio would say.

Mautusan knew the moment was fated, but he did not foresee that a girl child of high status would join his original party. So the eight of them, including four boatmen, embarked from Glidji in Mautusan's big canoe.

Now Mautusan's primary focus was wielding his way through the most dangerous part of their travels, which he surmised would take about three days. He did not want to alarm his mates, but he looked at the four pouches and put them away. He had eight muskets and powder, and the longboat, and with the human cargo, would be a prized catch if they fell into the unfriendly hands.

"How far are we from Cape Palmas," Adeoha said.

"We can be there in less than a moon if all goes well and the winds and currents favor us. But we have to be cautious and travel the river inlets, which may add a few days to our travels," Mautusan said.

As the longboat waved through the water, Mautusan stood upright and began to speak, not to anyone in particular, but they all could hear him, and they listened.

"It was not so difficult to avoid the slave vessels before because we knew where they were and the sea lanes they sailed. But now they are forced from their usual lines they could be lurking anywhere, so we'll stop here for the night."

At sunlight, the next day, Mautusan and his band began moving slowly through the marsh until they came upon a lake they were looking for; it would lead them to a waterway that would allow them to avoid the violent sea around the port of Aneho.

"This is the way to the lagoon, Tehseloh shouted. "You cannot see it, but I have been this way before. It has a small breadth, but we can follow it to the sea."

"Good, We'll stop here and rest the night. I'll go ahead with Tehseloh through the lagoon and see what, if anything, lays in wait. We don't want to encounter a slave brig smuggling human cargo near the shore. So arm yourselves with the muskets, and three of you keep watch at all times while the other three sleep.

Sitting around the ground with her mates in the evening sunlight, everyone occupied with their thoughts, Adeoha felt a cool wind despite the heat of that misty summer night. She has soured on life—all sweetness had gone. Was there anything left for her? She was prey to the circumstances that turned her life around so abruptly.

She pulled her three souls to her; herself and the Creator, and the ancestors, and it compelled her to look back to the day gone by when her life was held in the balance as she and her fellow travelers hid from the passing slave merchants.

It was her deeper self, her three souls opening a way for her. First, her eyes saw it, and then she felt it, tranquility; the rest of it she could not explain, a new day was coming, and her life would go on. And today, the beauty in the marshland awakened her to the beauty of life, no matter how difficult it gets at times.

Mautusan returned and informed them the coast was clear, and upon hearing it, they soon set out for the open sea, leaving behind one part of Afrika for another.

And in the other direction, on the sixth day after leaving Dahomey, the road from Allada to Atogon was loud with talk that the bokonon Eldeide had proclaimed that Adeoha's leaving Da's Belly had achieved a miracle.

And to Tubutu's delight, there were those along the road who spoke of King Guezo's speech taking due credit proclaiming his part in the matter before the crowd, and acknowledging Tubutu for bringing Adeoha, the cub lioness into the world, and relating the circumstances of her leaving to the oracle prophecy.

"Telling by the crackle in the people's voices, the incident has raised the King's popularity among them, and for me, it has allowed Adeoha to leave Da's Belly on a high note. It was a miracle, as Eldeide says, the way things happened and turned out to get Adeoha on the path to Cape Palmas," Tubutu thought.

"And why not? People like stories about magic because we could all use a little of it in our lives at times."

As Tubutu walked through Atogon, everyone greeted him along the way. Adeoha's age mates and those away from the road stopped what they were doing and waved to the band, with Oluwole and Tokou behind him happily receiving their new recognition.

When Tubutu walked through the compound gate, the first person who saw him was Lamtaala, and when he saw her in her simple, yellow dress and accessories that she wore when it was her week.

"I hoped it was your week, but prudence tells me it is not," Tubutu said.

"I have traded mine week with that of your second wife, so you will have to put up with Oshun and me the next four days. After we have eaten, Lady Glyya will take Oshun for the evening.

And Tubutu thanked Mawou-Lissa, Legba, and Fa, that his family and Ewansi's clan had weathered the storm, and there was peace in Da's Belly. Then he called Lamtaala, and they walked and talked their way through the compound toward his house, and somewhere along the way, Oshun spotted them, gave up her playing, and came running up beside them full of laughter.

*****

Adeoha's days at sea challenged her not unlike an adventure, except for leaving home. However, the nights were pleasant when not moving to avoid detection or searching for some mysterious water passage.

As they got closer to Cape Palmas, she learned from the Kroomen that the rivers were hard or impossible to navigate, but they had found large streams that sometimes, depending on the season, would admit the passage of Mautusan's longboats.

When the band did rest, it was in a relaxing place or at a longboat haven, and the Kroomen told their sea tales below the night sky and distant stars to the eagerly listening ears of Robert, Patricia, and Adeoha.

Near the end of the voyage, everyone thought all danger had passed as they neared Cape Palmas. Suddenly the light shower turned into furious squalls pushing the longboat into a stretch of heavy surf and treacherous undercurrents emanating when the torrent from the beach begins its travels to meet the tremendous waves of the sea. Now, they had encountered two separate forces reigning down on them at once.

Tehseloh and Gbwe shouted they had to make a run for it, so they sped through the dangerous pass, the pursuing heavy swells on one side, and the rushing waters in the passage to the ocean on the other, and both forces ready to engulf the unfortunate longboat at any moment.

They were fortunate the waters that formed its base on land was not more than two or three miles in breadth, or regardless of the Kroomen's skills or the longboat's speed; they would not have been able to survive the high breaking water much longer.

Once they reached Cape Palmas, Mautusan provided his three friends with accommodations at one of his estates. Robert and Patricia were anxious to continue their journey and finding the next boat to America and news about their friends, the Wheeler's. The first place the Wrinkles visited was the agency house and the Maryland Colonization Colony,

"There's a brig at the Pennsylvania Colony, now, and it will arrive in Cape Palmas in about a week," Dr. Lang said, who was in charge of the settlement.

"I can't believe it, just like that, we're going home," Patricia said.

"As for Reverend Wheeler and his wife, they're quite well. You can find their house at the North settlement." Dr. Lang said.

"There's a boat sailing from Cape Palmas in ten days for New York, Adeoha," Patricia said. "Robert and I will be on it."

"We will see; for now, I would like to learn about this country and its people," Adeoha said.

"You are now returning to your country with wealth in your hand," Mautusan said to Robert as they walked along the shore.

"Patricia and I discussed the matter just recently, the hardship of returning home with nothing in hand, all our friends and everyone will have five or six years on us to start new careers and businesses or take on new professions," Robert said.

The next day, Robert, Patricia, and Adeoha received an invite from the Reverend and Mrs. Wheeler for supper."

Adeoha bowed before both the Wheeler's in turn, "I feel that I have met with you many times through conversations with Lady Patricia," Adeoha said. She explained to me how you created a Grebo alphabet and dictionary. I feel you can create a Dahomean alphabet? If one knows the alphabet, all the things I have learned can be taught to anyone who knows the Dahomean alphabet.

"I suppose I could, I think we'll be leaving Cape Palmas soon for another Afrikan country, and I'm going to have to create an alphabet for the peoples of that country soon," Reverend Wheeler said.

"We are very proud of the thirty-eight Mena who have completed their education at the mission schools we established. And we've been able to translate into printed books Grebo portions of the bible, school books, and hymns, thanks to our good friend and colleague, Reverend Woodrow Miles, who came to us with a printing press," Mrs. Wheeler said.

Adeoha hardly spoke at the Wheeler's gathering, but her interest in Reverend Miles grew because he was a black man born and raised in America and a priest of status. So she sought him out after supper, and they arranged to have lunch two days later.

"I will focus on what is necessary for a big business in this country, Adeoha thought. The Grebo teachers at the school know the yovo language as I do, and from them, I can learn Grebo and converse with the people in their language.

"The yovo and the black settlers seem to have several colonies like the one that brought Robert and Patricia to Afrika. I can make good business in these markets, stretching from here to Monrovia and beyond.

Two days passed, Adeoha looked across the table at Reverend Miles, a young man, maybe a score and ten in age, a coffee-brown hue and chesty physique.

"If I decide to come to America, tell me how everyone will treat my business," Adeoha said in surprise as she spoke the words coming to America for the first time."

"These things that you ask are happening now; men and women of color and whites are working in accord for the good of all from whatever station in life that maintains them, Reverend Miles said.

"Like any battle for independence, there will be both good days and bad, but the new ground is broken enough and finds its way into our laws and politics, education and religion. And abolishing slavery and women's rights have joined forces, seeing colored newspapers and organizations. And white people and Negroes are doing these things together."

Adeoha found her talk with Reverend Miles a good learning experience. It brought forth an idea: the mountain of different courses and activities and movements in America she would be thrown amidst if she were there. But today, she wanted to meet some of the black settlers from America and hear their thoughts on the conflict with the native people.

Many of the Americans she talked with, including former slaves, set free only on the condition they come to Afrika, seem to have a great longing for the country they left behind. Some were looking for a new start, while still others felt their lives couldn't be any worse.

"I did not have to look for conversation with the black chiefs of the American settlers," Adeoha thought. "On separate occasions in my short time here, they have sought me out for discourse. I sense they come to find what my intentions are. They remind me of the social descent between notables and commoners in Dahomey."

Adeoha hired a young man who was a teacher at the mission school to accompany her when she conversed with the Mena and translate English and Grebo between them.

One day Adeoha planted crops with the women, and when the day was over, they were only too happy to talk with her about their lives. The talk was mostly about how the black Americans from across the sea had bought their land and looked to rule their lives.

She learned from the women and men of the Mena; they had the money to buy the goods she would sell. She also learned of twelve white towns, the furthest not far from where she stood. So between the yovo and the black chiefs, and the common settlers and the native people. I can have a good business in Cape Palmas.

"As yet, I have not found in Cape Palmas, the people of extravagant wealth and their sons and daughters, for only they can afford my expensive goods.

"Cape Palmas also has not the trading towns like Da's Belly or a place where goods come from across the sea like locusts and fill the land with cowries and everything else under the sun, both good and bad.

"What have I learned about America? Adeoha thought. I can say by the people I know from there, Robert naïve and Patricia viovi, the Reverend and Mrs. Wheeler, who I have just met, but I hold on high because their hearts are with the people, and they understand much.

"And the Reverend Miles holds influence on me, seeing the status he has reached as a black man in America, and hearing him speak of so many others, whites, and blacks, who are coming together.

The next day, Adeoha went to see Robert and Patricia, catching them just as they were leaving for an eatery they liked in White Town, and she joined them in their carriage ride.

"I have decided to come to America with you. Your country is too mischievous, too big, and too in the middle of everything for me not to avail myself of it.

"You know how happy I am, just the thought of you in the United States, and now we'll be together, at least until you make plans," Patricia said. "

"Come, ladies, let's ride the shore this evening and relish that we have made it to this point, and look forward to our travels to America without incident," Robert said.

"Yes, I am here. It does no good to look back; I am confident going forward," Adeoha said.

The long vessel arrived at Cape Palmas the next day. And three days later, the friends stood together on the shoreline saying farewell, but most of it was for

Mautusan, for the three of them would not see him again.

"It came as a blessing from Mawou Lissa that the two of you [Robert and Patricia] came to Cape Palmas, and if that wasn't enough, you came into my life and pushed me to return to Dahomey. I made plenty of cowries and grew expensive things there, which you knew nothing about until recently, but it was safer that way for us both, Mautusan said.

"I did, however, get some satisfaction at running my business right under Guezo's nose. But it only reminded me of the wrong done to my family. I got a chance to return for a while to the land of my birth and see old friends.

"No sense in me tempting the hands of fate, I will keep out of the Bights of Benin for now and sail the waters around the Cape and the windward.

"And I will not forget you, Mautusan," Robert and Patricia said in the same breath, and they both embraced him. "Our years in Dahomey have been amazing."

"Robert and I have found in Afrika all the possibilities of greatness and wonder we imagined, and we owe that to you. But now, I look forward to going home and returning to the people's struggles I left behind when I came to Afrika.

"In uncounted ways," Adeoha said, "as she walked toward Mautusan in playful gist, "my life changed when you came with the yovo couple to Dahomey. May Legba keep you safe from trouble and watch your way at life's crossroads."

Mautusan looked at Adeoha in wonder and spoke, "Were you the reason the three of us [Robert and Patricia, and Mautusan] came to Da's Belly? And then he laughed. "The people of Dahomey will talk about the things that happened to us and the oracle story for a long time. It has the makings of a good tale with the King and nobles and high ranking officials as adversaries."

In 1841, fourteenth of February, the brig Raven set sail for New York under Captain Longpool. It carried a full cargo of palm oil and timber and six passengers, three of whom were Robert and Patricia Wringle and Adeoha Adetoye.

As the vessel forged ahead and the shores of Afrika had long disappeared from view, Adeoha looked up at the patches of blue sky and white clouds. Then she gazed into the distance where Afrika was, though she could no longer see it.

Instead, she saw a breathtaking scene of all the colors of the sky above the now invisible Afrika, guiding the traveler to its shore. And she thought of Aido Hwedo, or Damballa, the sacred rainbow serpent. And she thought of the ancient ancestors, the Yeveh and the Tchamba, whose help and guidance she would require in this new country.